JURASSIC PARK

™

VOLUME 9

ANIMALS VS. GODS!

ADAPTED BY
STEVE ENGLEHART
CHAZ TRUOG
AND PAUL FRICKE

Spotlight

IDW
™

visit us at www.abdopublishing.com

Reinforced library bound editions published in 2014 by Spotlight, a division of the ABDO Group, PO Box 398166, Minneapolis, Minnesota 55439. Published by agreement with IDW Publishing. www.idwpublishing.com

Printed in the United States of America, North Mankato, Minnesota.
052013
092013
♻ This book contains at least 10% recycled materials.

Library of Congress Cataloging-in-Publication Data

Englehart, Steve.
 Jurassic Park / adapted by Steve Englehart, Armand Gil, and Dell Barras. -- Reinforced library edition.
      pages cm. -- (Jurassic Park ; v. 5-10)
   Summary: "Three days after their escape from Isla Nublar, Dr. Alan Grant and Dr. Ellie Sattler have returned to help confine the dinosaurs. When the escaped raptors remain elusive, Grant and Sattler go on their own mission... and discover they aren't the only ones looking for raptors!"-- Provided by publisher.
   ISBN 978-1-61479-187-4 (vol. 5: Aftershocks!) -- ISBN 978-1-61479-188-1 (vol. 6: Dark cargo!) -- ISBN 978-1-61479-189-8 (vol. 7: Raptors attack) -- ISBN 978-1-61479-190-4 (vol. 8: Animals vs. men) -- ISBN 978-1-61479-191-1 (vol. 9: Animals vs. gods!) -- ISBN 978-1-61479-192-8 (vol. 10: Gods vs. men!)
   1. Graphic novels. [1. Graphic novels. 2. Dinosaurs--Fiction. 3. Science fiction.] I. Gil, Armand. II. Barras, Dell. III. Title.
   PZ7.7.E6Jur 2013
   741.5'973--dc23
                                            2013013372

All Spotlight books are reinforced library binding and manufactured in the United States of America.

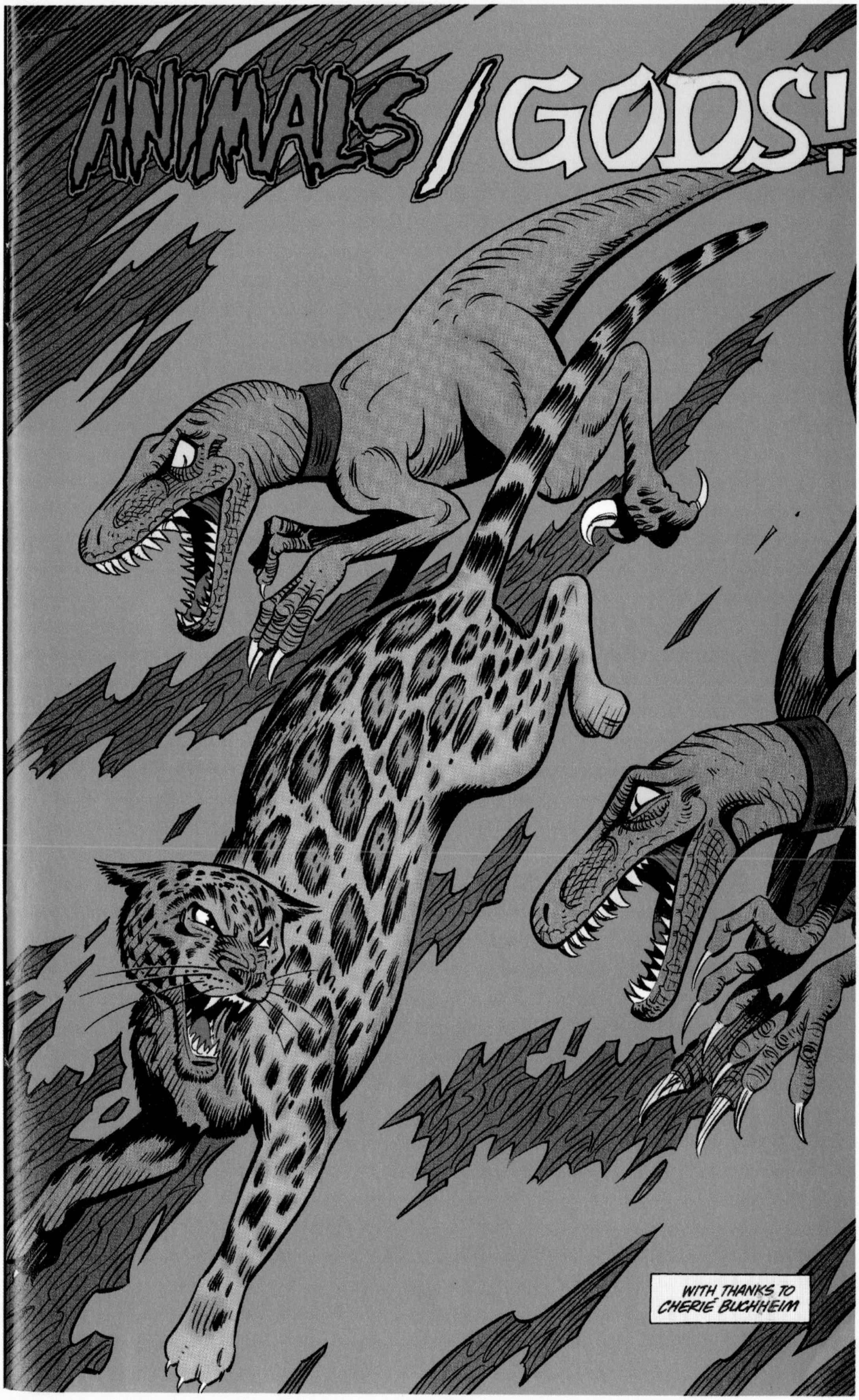
ANIMALS / GODS!
WITH THANKS TO
CHERIÉ BUCHHEIM

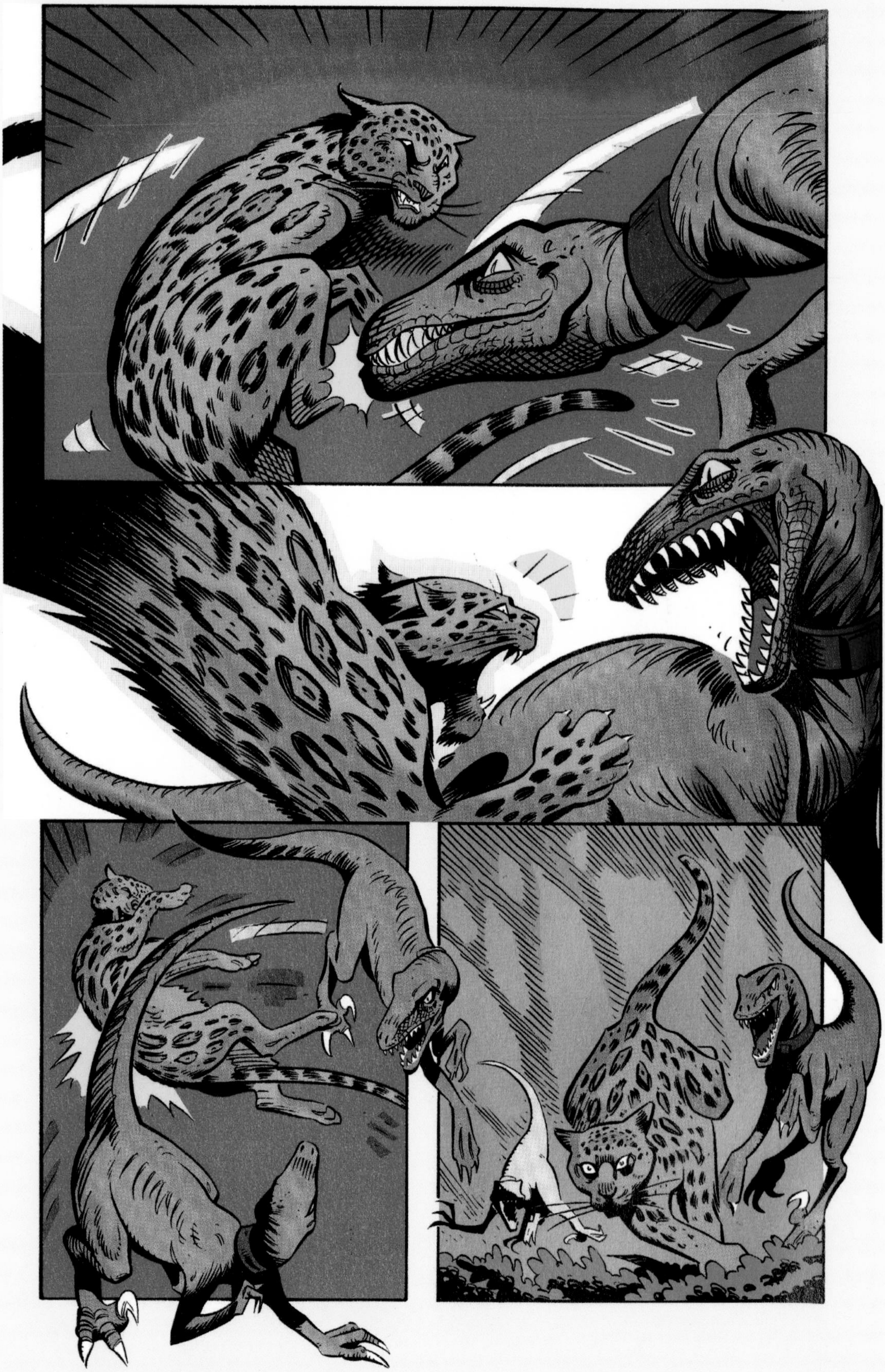

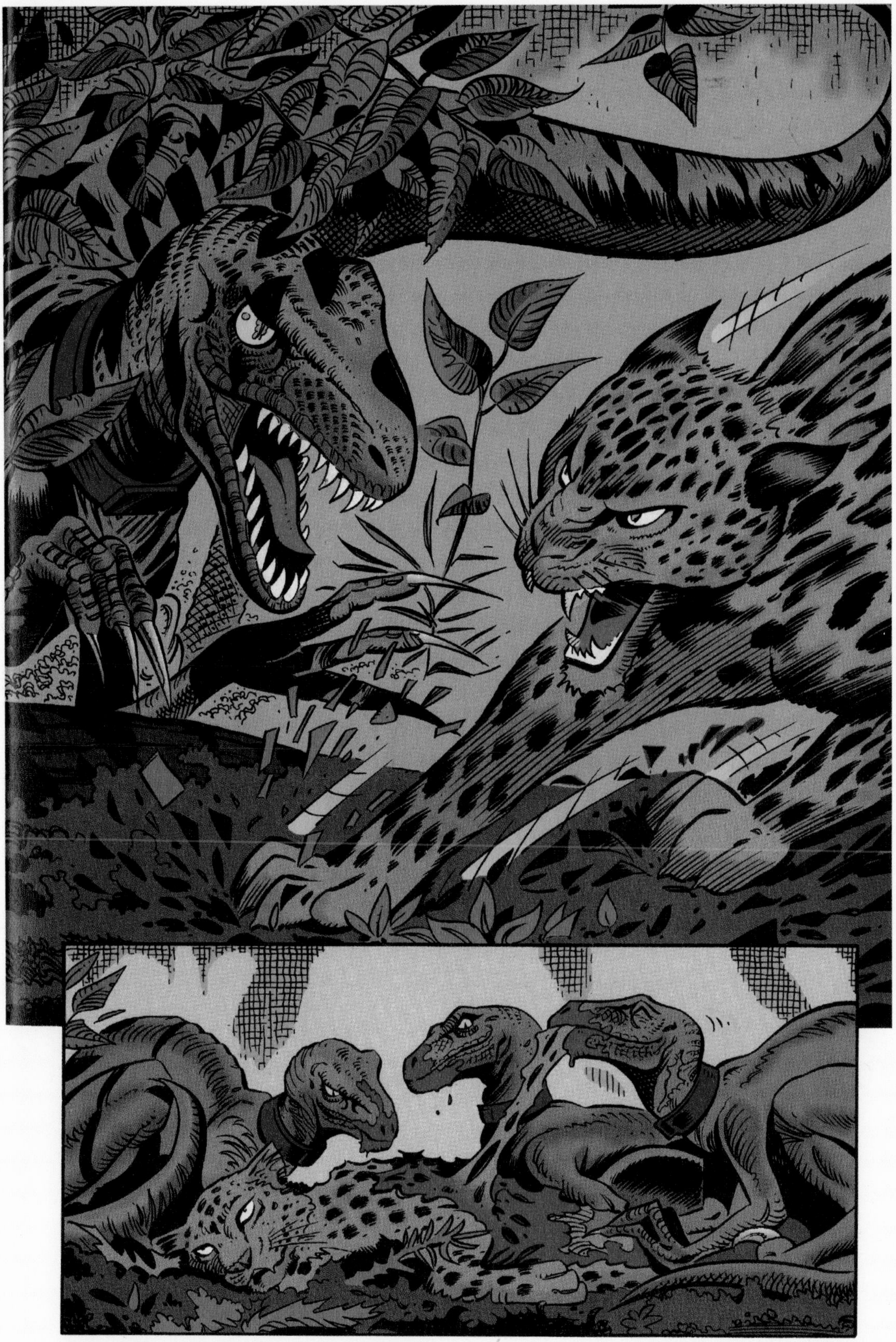
IT'S GOOD TO BE FREE AND WILD AGAIN...

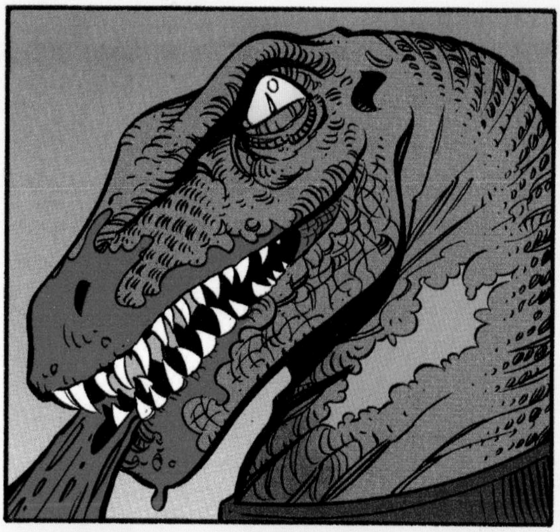

THE THREE RAPTORS, NICKNAMED *ALF* AND *BETTY* AND *CELIA* BY ALAN GRANT AND ELLIE SATTLER, WERE *HATCHED* FREE BUT ALMOST IMMEDIATELY *CAPTURED!* TODAY IS THE *FIRST* DAY THEY'VE EATEN FOOD *THEY CAUGHT!*

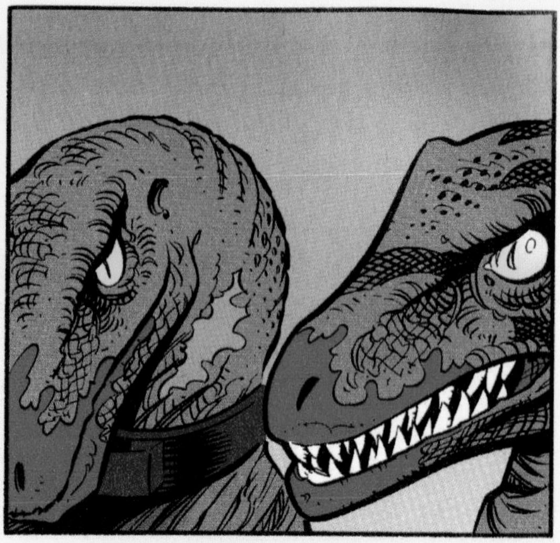

ALF AND *BETTY* WERE FORCED TO *DEVELOP* THEIR HUNTING SKILLS BY THAT DARK-HAIRED MAN, BUT *CELIA* WAS KEPT *TIED UP* WHILE THE BIG *CUT* IN HER NECK GOT *BETTER!*

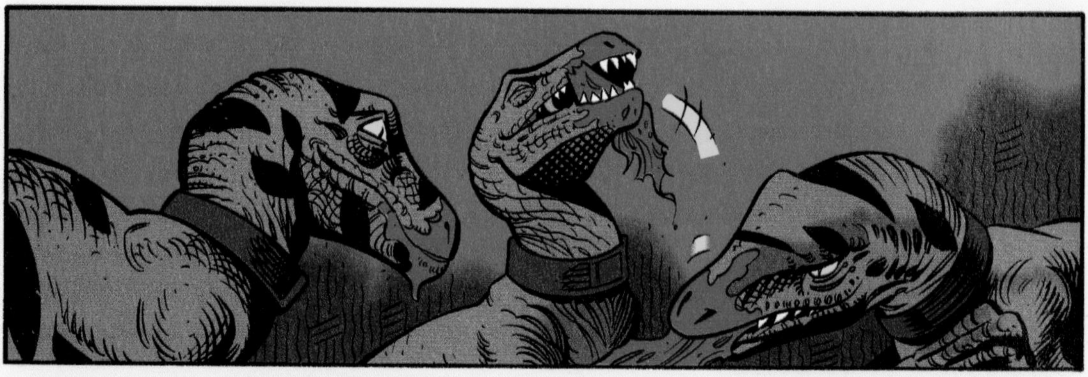

HER BROTHER AND SISTER ARE *PLEASED* WITH HOW *WELL* SHE *WORKED* WITH THEM! THESE THREE ARE *FINE* KILLERS!

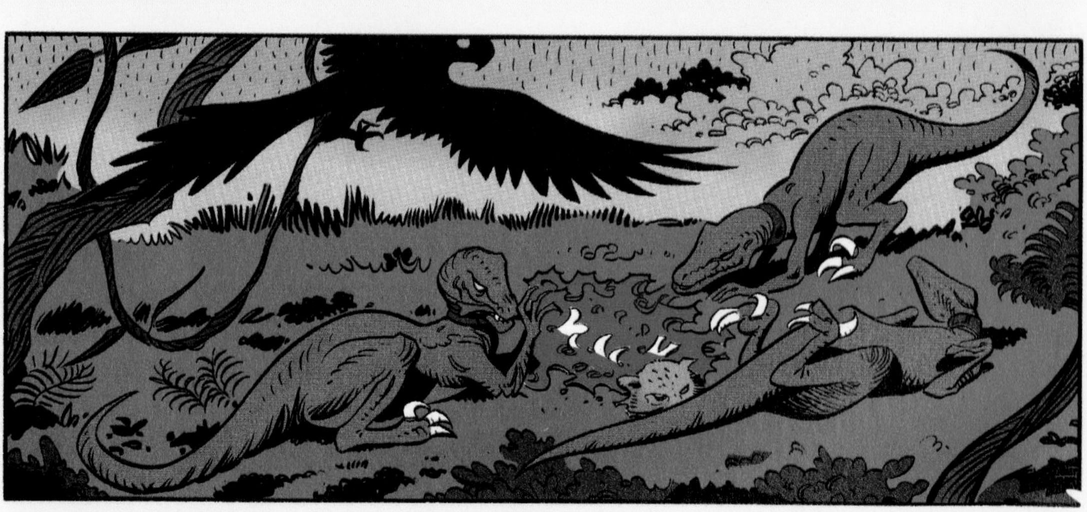

IT'S *GOOD* TO BE FREE AND WILD AND *SIMPLE* AGAIN...

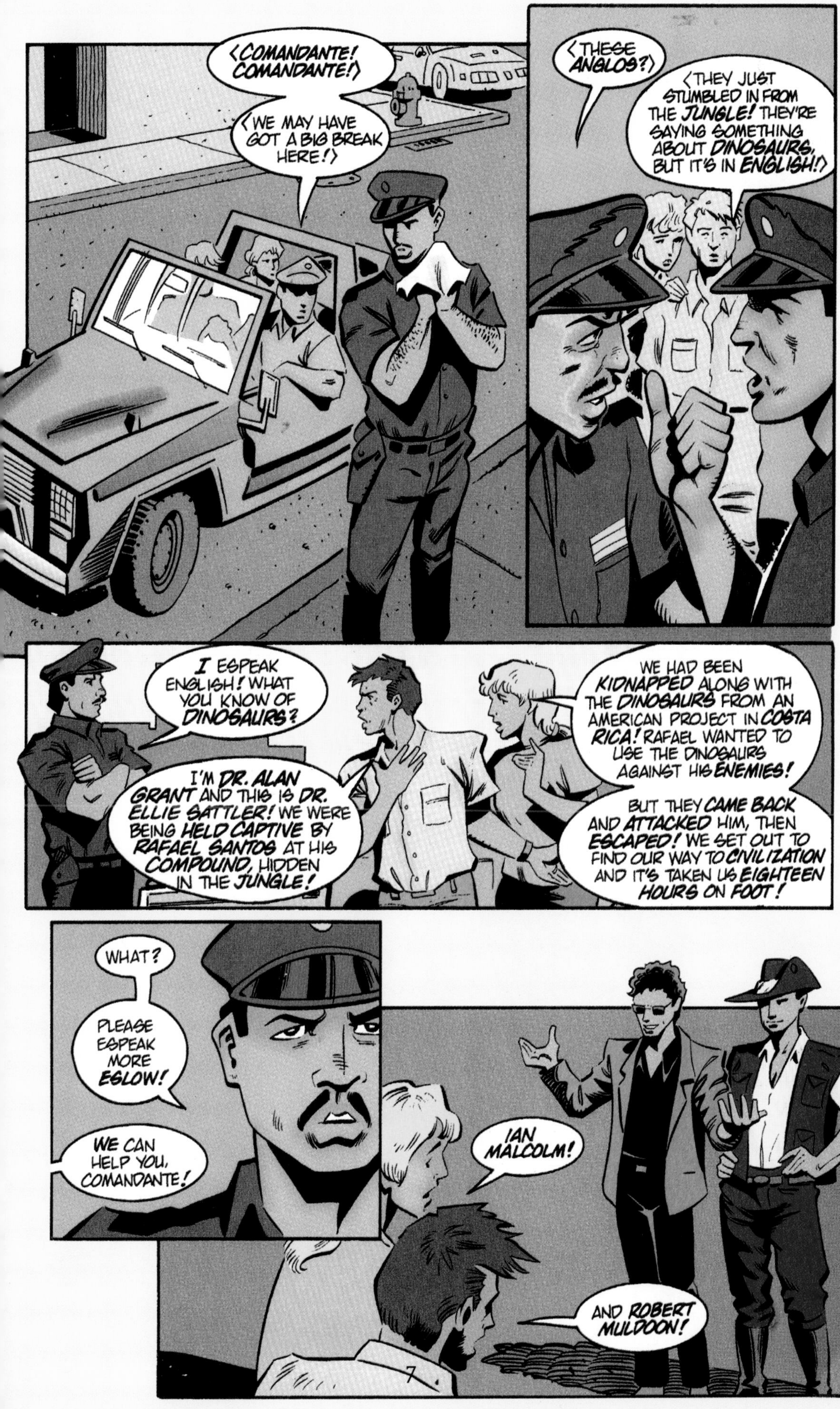

<COMANDANTE! COMANDANTE!>
<WE MAY HAVE GOT A BIG BREAK HERE!>
<THESE ANGLOS?>
<THEY JUST STUMBLED IN FROM THE JUNGLE! THEY'RE SAYING SOMETHING ABOUT DINOSAURS, BUT IT'S IN ENGLISH!>
I ESPEAK ENGLISH! WHAT YOU KNOW OF DINOSAURS?
I'M DR. ALAN GRANT AND THIS IS DR. ELLIE SATTLER! WE WERE BEING HELD CAPTIVE BY RAFAEL SANTOS AT HIS COMPOUND, HIDDEN IN THE JUNGLE!
WE HAD BEEN KIDNAPPED ALONG WITH THE DINOSAURS FROM AN AMERICAN PROJECT IN COSTA RICA! RAFAEL WANTED TO USE THE DINOSAURS AGAINST HIS ENEMIES!
BUT THEY CAME BACK AND ATTACKED HIM, THEN ESCAPED! WE SET OUT TO FIND OUR WAY TO CIVILIZATION AND IT'S TAKEN US EIGHTEEN HOURS ON FOOT!
WHAT?
PLEASE ESPEAK MORE ESLOW!
WE CAN HELP YOU, COMANDANTE!
IAN MALCOLM!
AND ROBERT MULDOON!

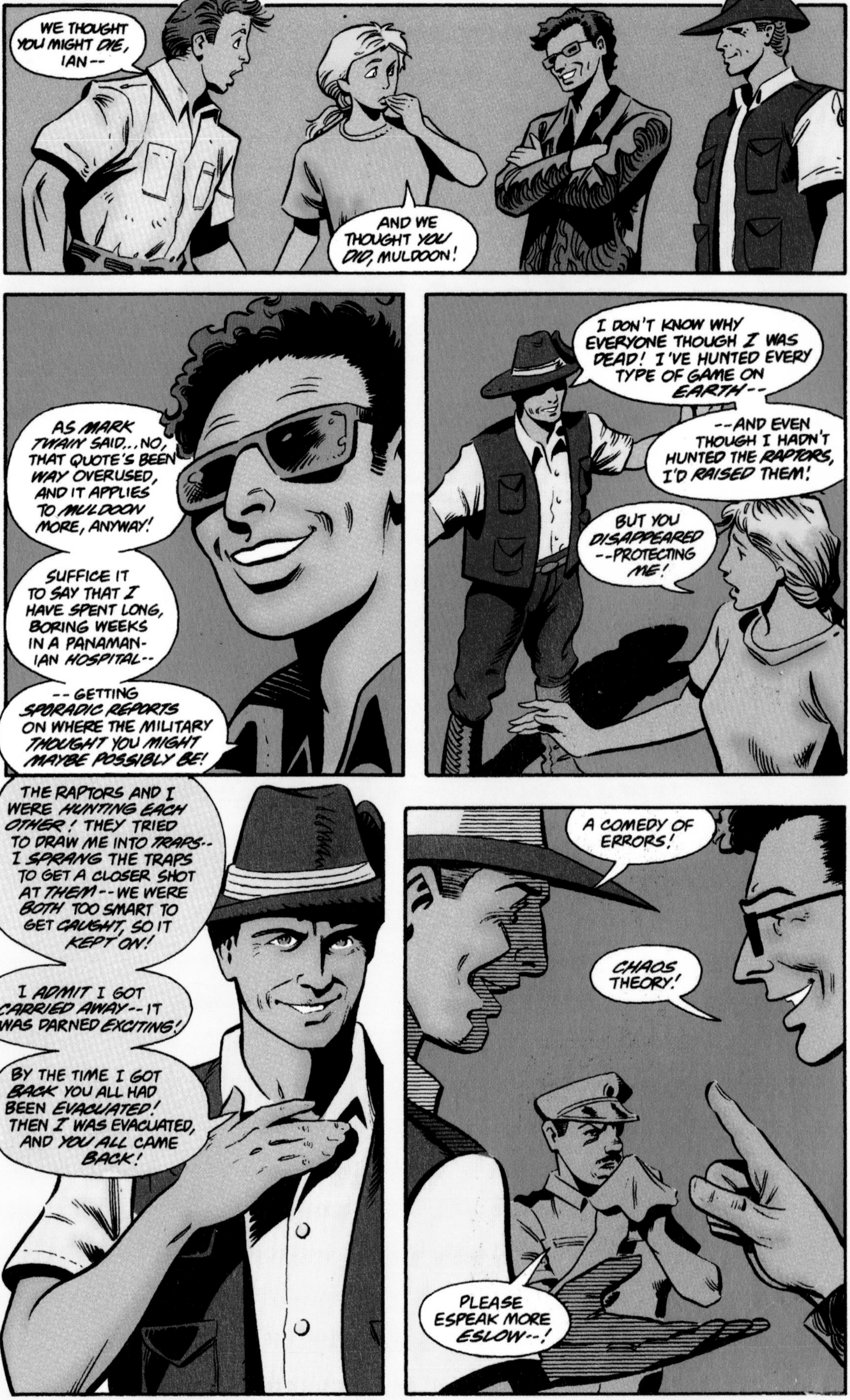
WE THOUGHT YOU MIGHT DIE, IAN--
AND WE THOUGHT YOU DID, MULDOON!
AS MARK TWAIN SAID... NO, THAT QUOTE'S BEEN WAY OVERUSED, AND IT APPLIES TO MULDOON MORE, ANYWAY!
SUFFICE IT TO SAY THAT I HAVE SPENT LONG, BORING WEEKS IN A PANAMANIAN HOSPITAL--
--GETTING SPORADIC REPORTS ON WHERE THE MILITARY THOUGHT YOU MIGHT MAYBE POSSIBLY BE!
I DON'T KNOW WHY EVERYONE THOUGH I WAS DEAD! I'VE HUNTED EVERY TYPE OF GAME ON EARTH--
--AND EVEN THOUGH I HADN'T HUNTED THE RAPTORS, I'D RAISED THEM!
BUT YOU DISAPPEARED --PROTECTING ME!
THE RAPTORS AND I WERE HUNTING EACH OTHER! THEY TRIED TO DRAW ME INTO TRAPS-- I SPRANG THE TRAPS TO GET A CLOSER SHOT AT THEM--WE WERE BOTH TOO SMART TO GET CAUGHT, SO IT KEPT ON!
I ADMIT I GOT CARRIED AWAY--IT WAS DARNED EXCITING!
BY THE TIME I GOT BACK YOU ALL HAD BEEN EVACUATED! THEN I WAS EVACUATED, AND YOU ALL CAME BACK!
A COMEDY OF ERRORS!
CHAOS THEORY!
PLEASE ESPEAK MORE ESLOW--!

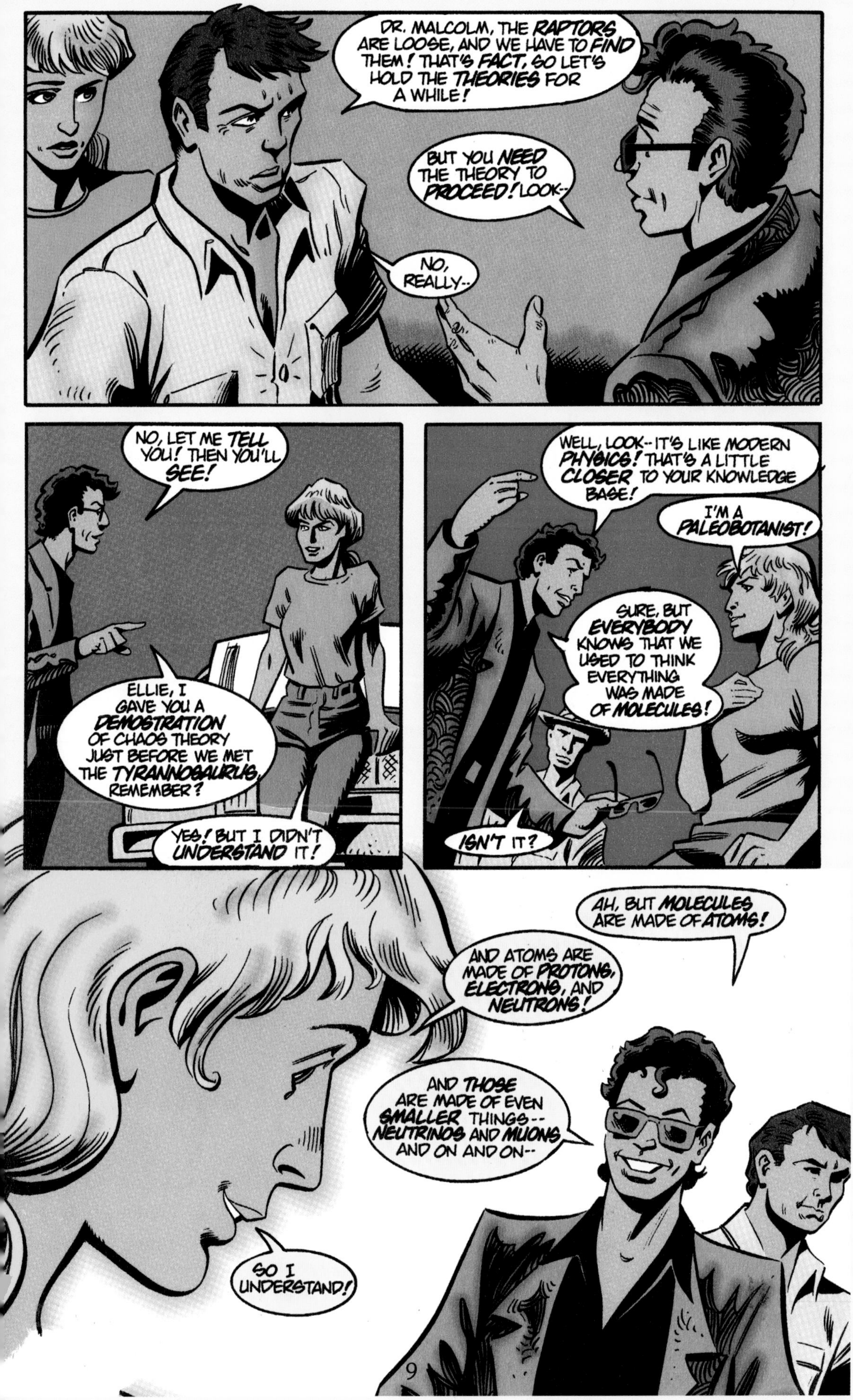
DR. MALCOLM, THE RAPTORS ARE LOOSE, AND WE HAVE TO FIND THEM! THAT'S FACT, SO LET'S HOLD THE THEORIES FOR A WHILE!
BUT YOU NEED THE THEORY TO PROCEED! LOOK--
NO, REALLY--
NO, LET ME TELL YOU! THEN YOU'LL SEE!
ELLIE, I GAVE YOU A DEMOSTRATION OF CHAOS THEORY JUST BEFORE WE MET THE TYRANNOSAURUS, REMEMBER?
YES! BUT I DIDN'T UNDERSTAND IT!
WELL, LOOK-- IT'S LIKE MODERN PHYSICS! THAT'S A LITTLE CLOSER TO YOUR KNOWLEDGE BASE!
I'M A PALEOBOTANIST!
SURE, BUT EVERYBODY KNOWS THAT WE USED TO THINK EVERYTHING WAS MADE OF MOLECULES!
ISN'T IT?
AH, BUT MOLECULES ARE MADE OF ATOMS!
AND ATOMS ARE MADE OF PROTONS, ELECTRONS, AND NEUTRONS!
AND THOSE ARE MADE OF EVEN SMALLER THINGS-- NEUTRINOS AND MUONS AND ON AND ON--
SO I UNDERSTAND!

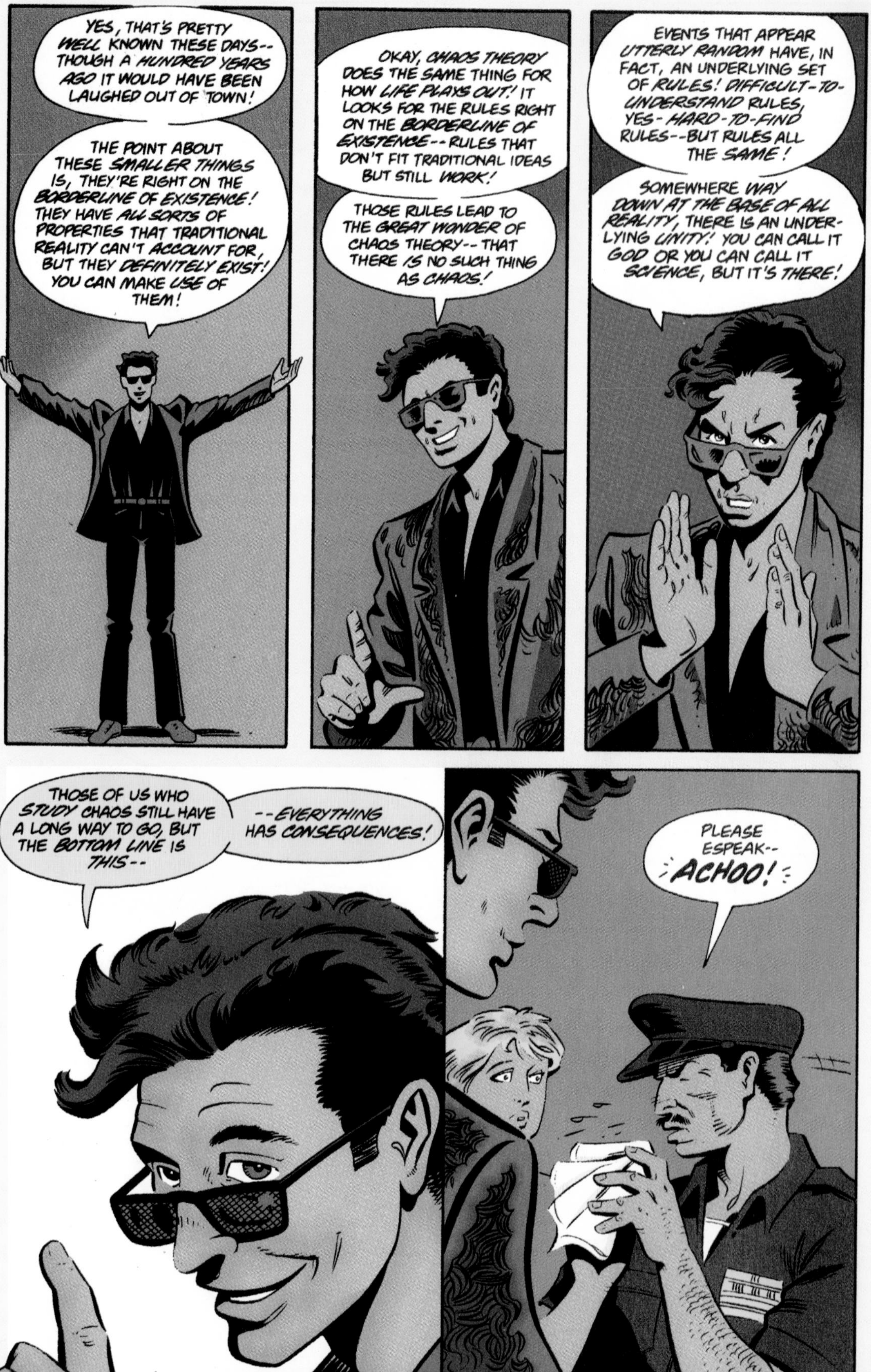
YES, THAT'S PRETTY WELL KNOWN THESE DAYS-- THOUGH A HUNDRED YEARS AGO IT WOULD HAVE BEEN LAUGHED OUT OF TOWN!
THE POINT ABOUT THESE SMALLER THINGS IS, THEY'RE RIGHT ON THE BORDERLINE OF EXISTENCE! THEY HAVE ALL SORTS OF PROPERTIES THAT TRADITIONAL REALITY CAN'T ACCOUNT FOR, BUT THEY DEFINITELY EXIST! YOU CAN MAKE USE OF THEM!
OKAY, CHAOS THEORY DOES THE SAME THING FOR HOW LIFE PLAYS OUT! IT LOOKS FOR THE RULES RIGHT ON THE BORDERLINE OF EXISTENCE--RULES THAT DON'T FIT TRADITIONAL IDEAS BUT STILL WORK!
THOSE RULES LEAD TO THE GREAT WONDER OF CHAOS THEORY-- THAT THERE IS NO SUCH THING AS CHAOS!
EVENTS THAT APPEAR UTTERLY RANDOM HAVE, IN FACT, AN UNDERLYING SET OF RULES! DIFFICULT-TO-UNDERSTAND RULES, YES- HARD-TO-FIND RULES--BUT RULES ALL THE SAME!
SOMEWHERE WAY DOWN AT THE BASE OF ALL REALITY, THERE IS AN UNDERLYING UNITY! YOU CAN CALL IT GOD OR YOU CAN CALL IT SCIENCE, BUT IT'S THERE!
THOSE OF US WHO STUDY CHAOS STILL HAVE A LONG WAY TO GO, BUT THE BOTTOM LINE IS THIS--
--EVERYTHING HAS CONSEQUENCES!
PLEASE ESPEAK-- ACHOO!

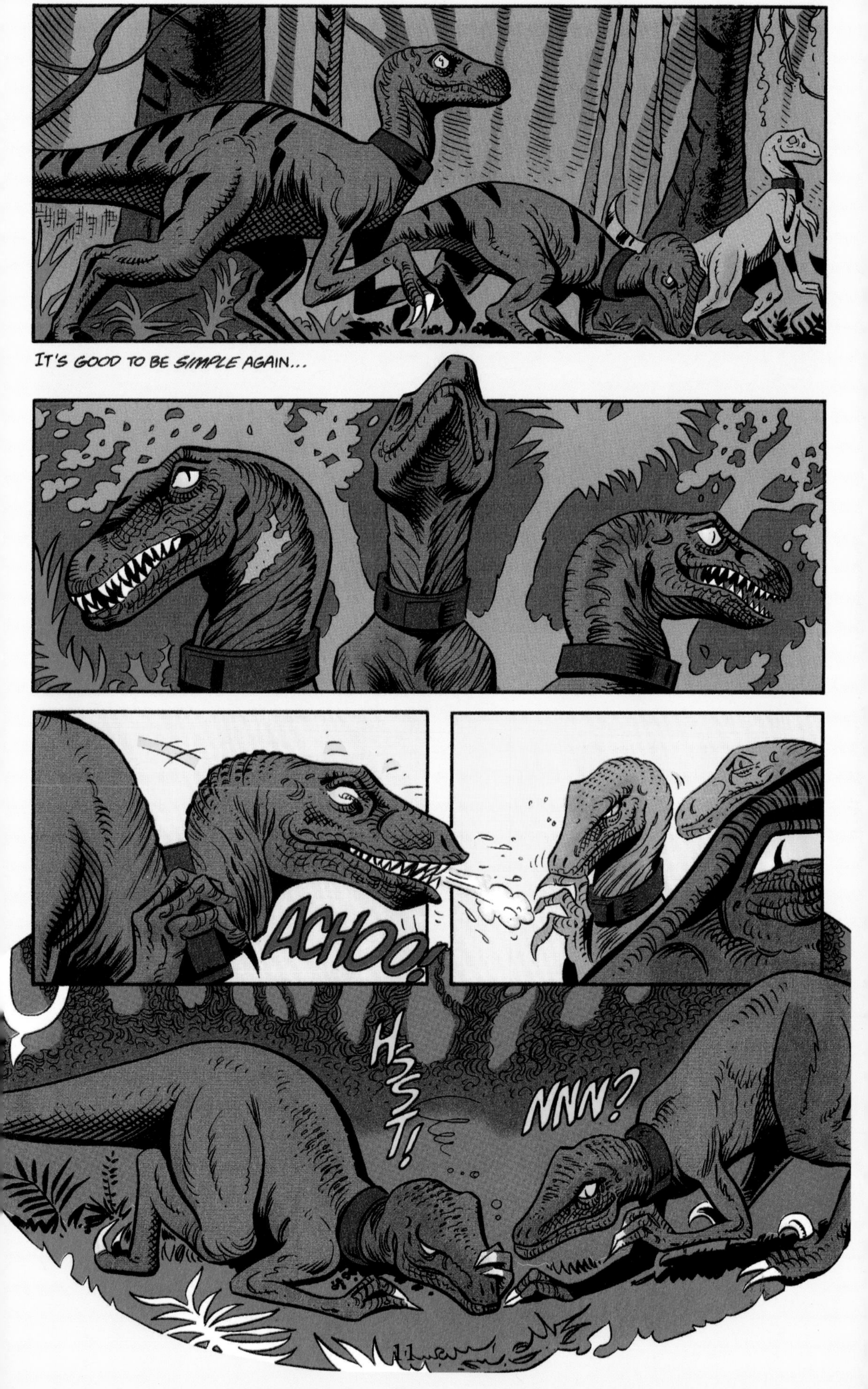
IT'S GOOD TO BE *SIMPLE* AGAIN...
ACHOO!
HSST!
NNN?

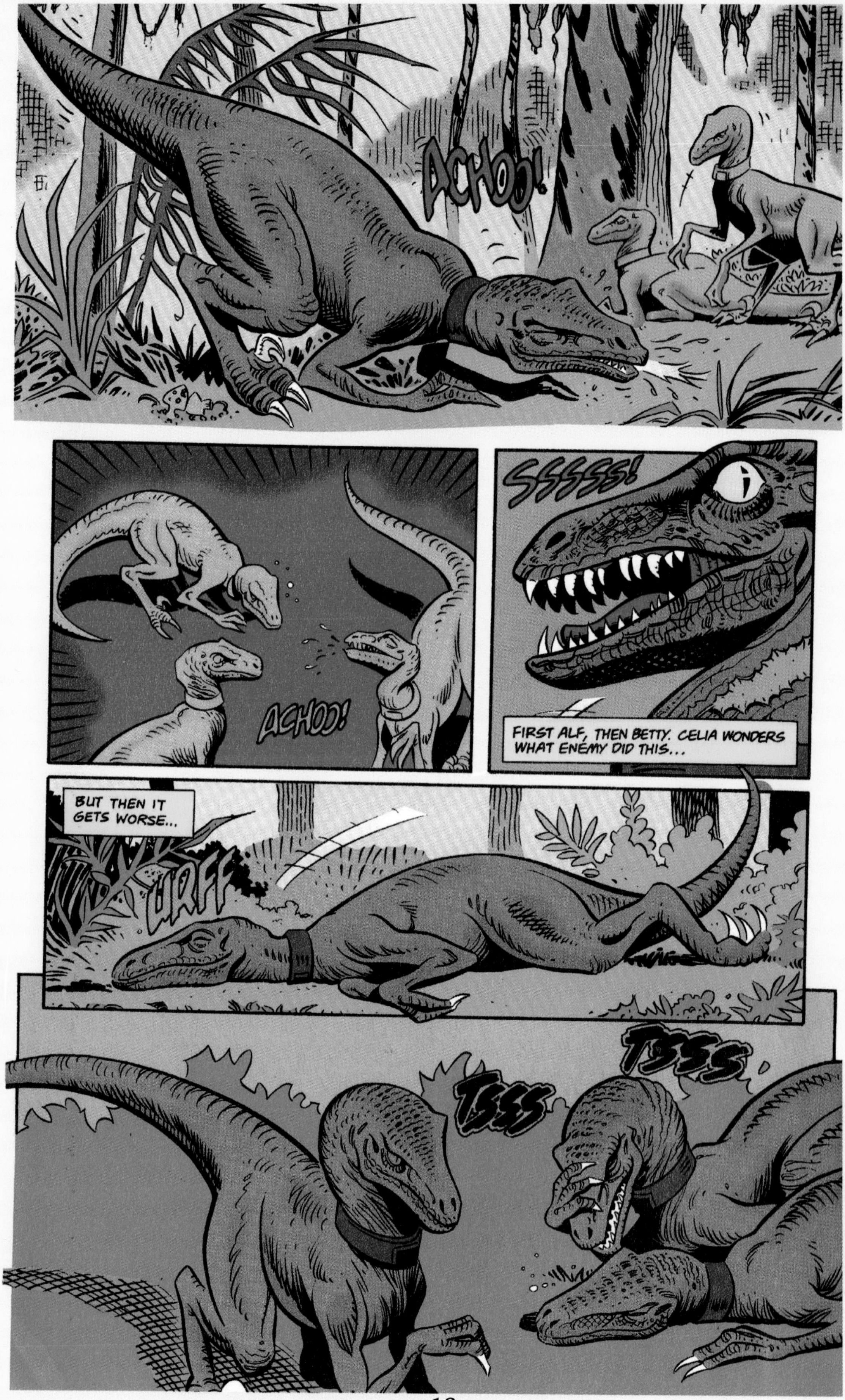
ACHOO!
ACHOO!
SSSSSS!
FIRST ALF, THEN BETTY. CELIA WONDERS WHAT ENEMY DID THIS...
BUT THEN IT GETS WORSE...
URFF
TSSS
TSSS

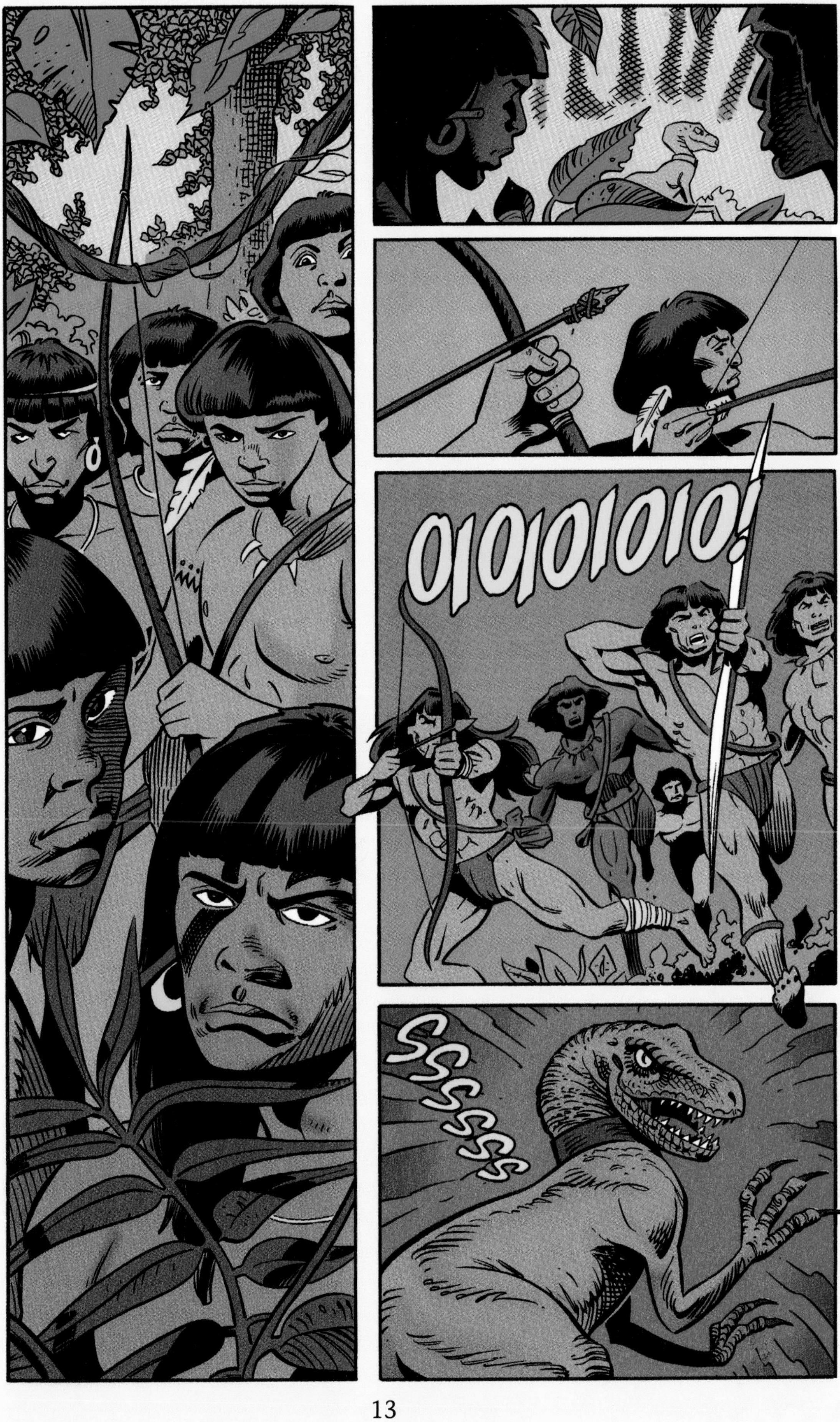
OIOIOIOIOIO!
SSSSSS

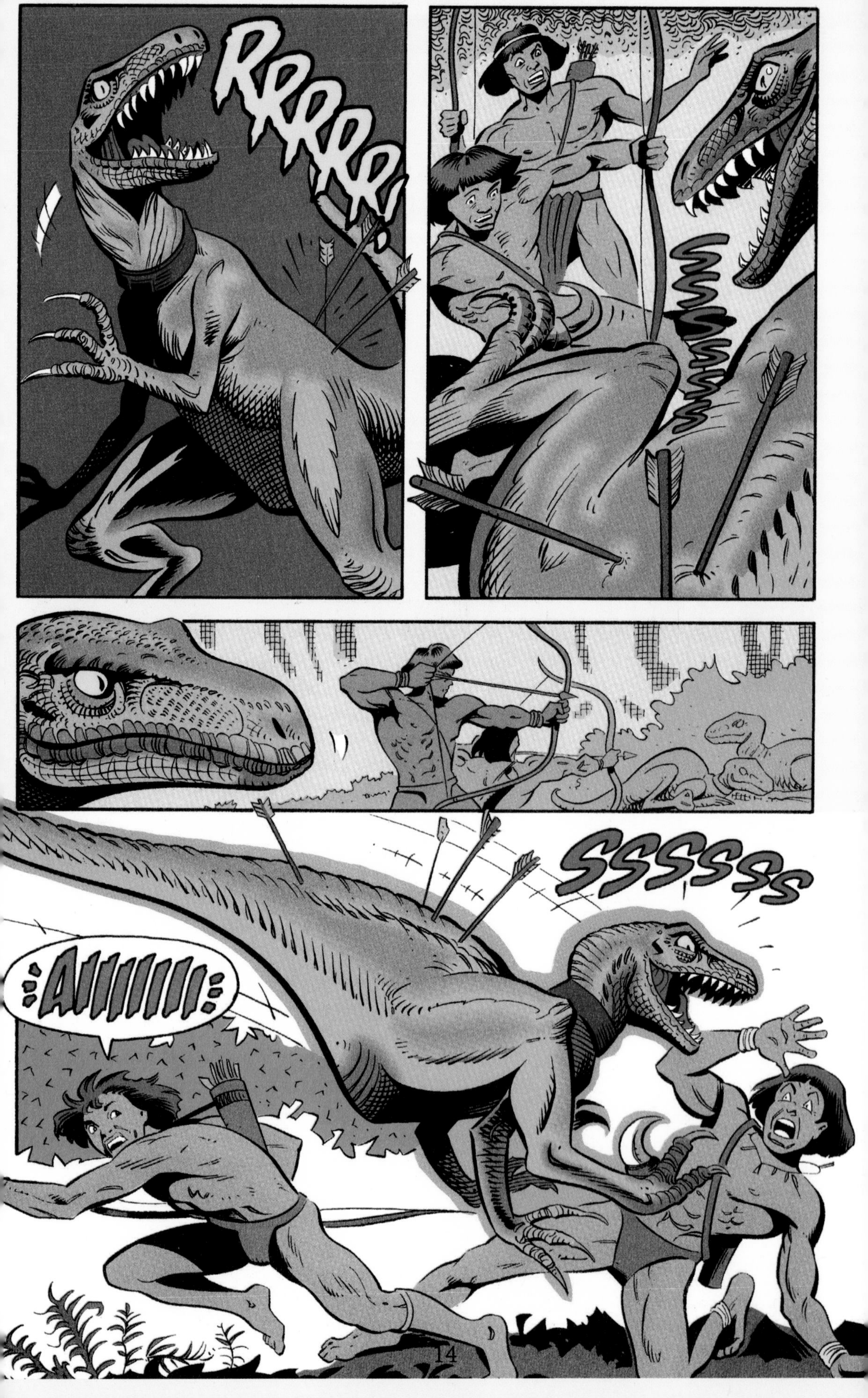
RRRRR!
SSSSSS
AIIIIIII!

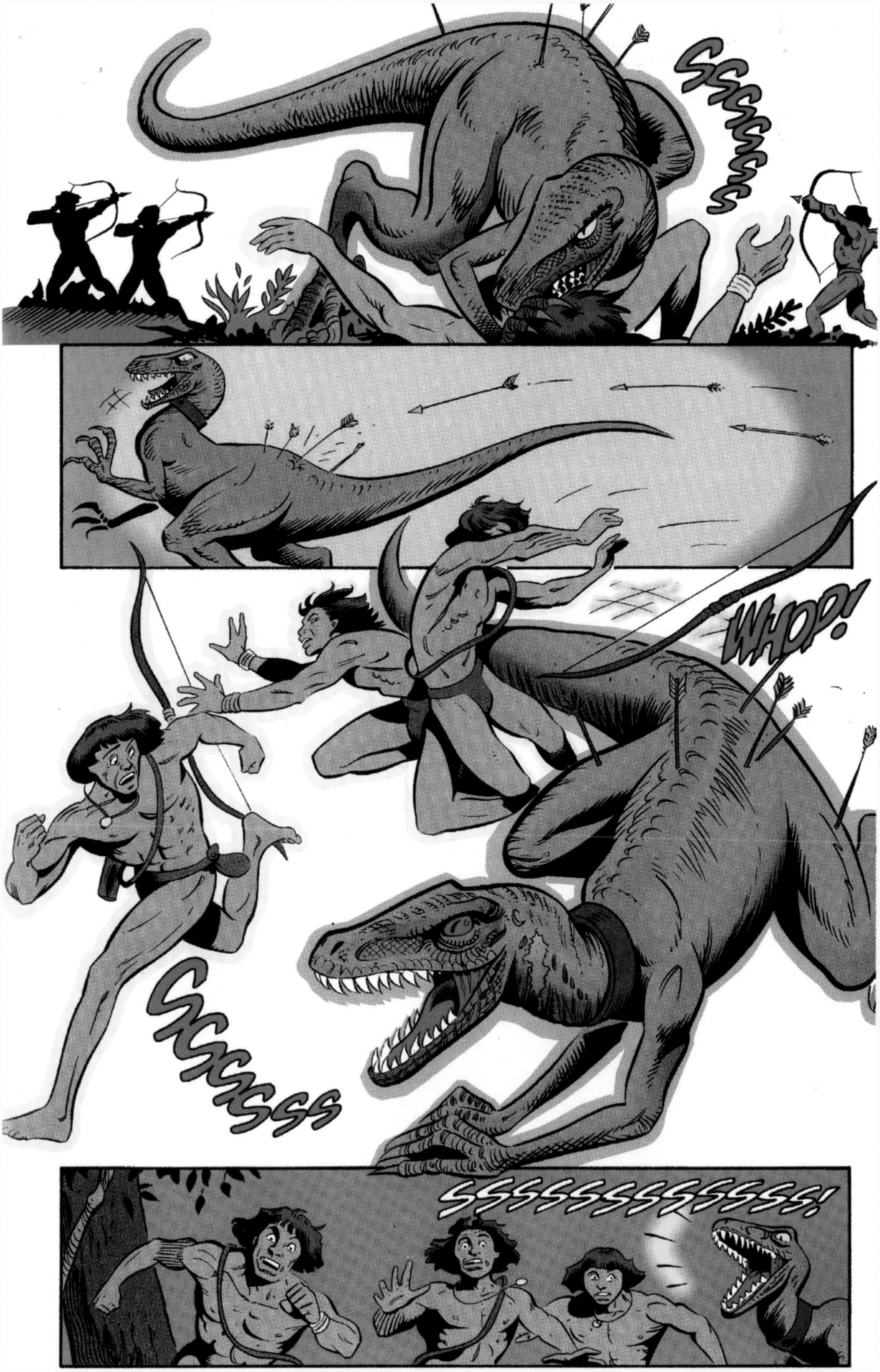
SSSSSSSS
WHOP!
SSSSSSS
SSSSSSSSSSSSSSS!

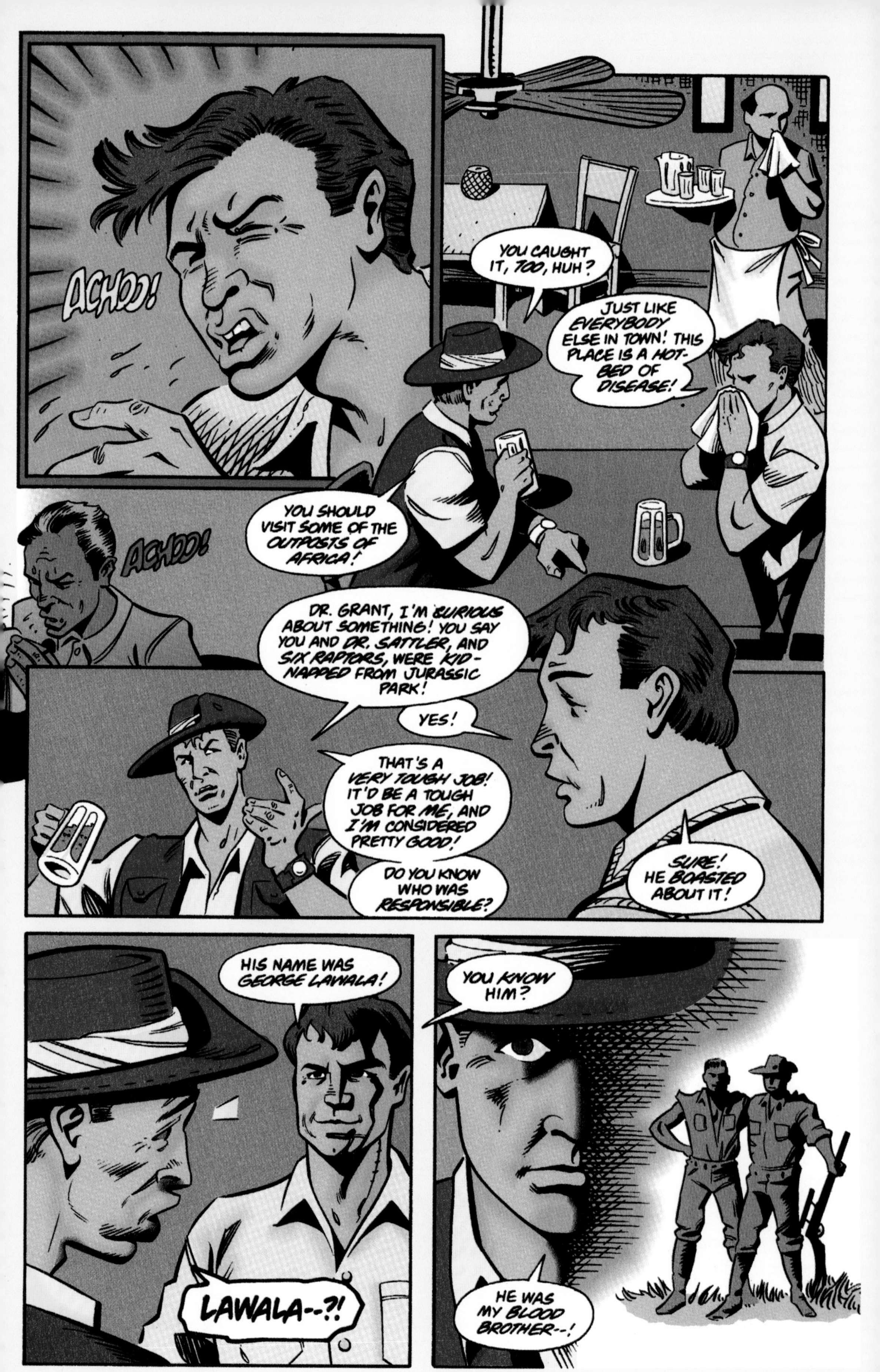
ACHOO!
YOU CAUGHT IT, TOO, HUH?
JUST LIKE EVERYBODY ELSE IN TOWN! THIS PLACE IS A HOT-BED OF DISEASE!
YOU SHOULD VISIT SOME OF THE OUTPOSTS OF AFRICA!
ACHOO!
DR. GRANT, I'M CURIOUS ABOUT SOMETHING! YOU SAY YOU AND DR. SATTLER, AND SIX RAPTORS, WERE KID-NAPPED FROM JURASSIC PARK!
YES!
THAT'S A VERY TOUGH JOB! IT'D BE A TOUGH JOB FOR ME, AND I'M CONSIDERED PRETTY GOOD!
DO YOU KNOW WHO WAS RESPONSIBLE?
SURE! HE BOASTED ABOUT IT!
HIS NAME WAS GEORGE LAWALA!
LAWALA--?!
YOU KNOW HIM?
HE WAS MY BLOOD BROTHER--!

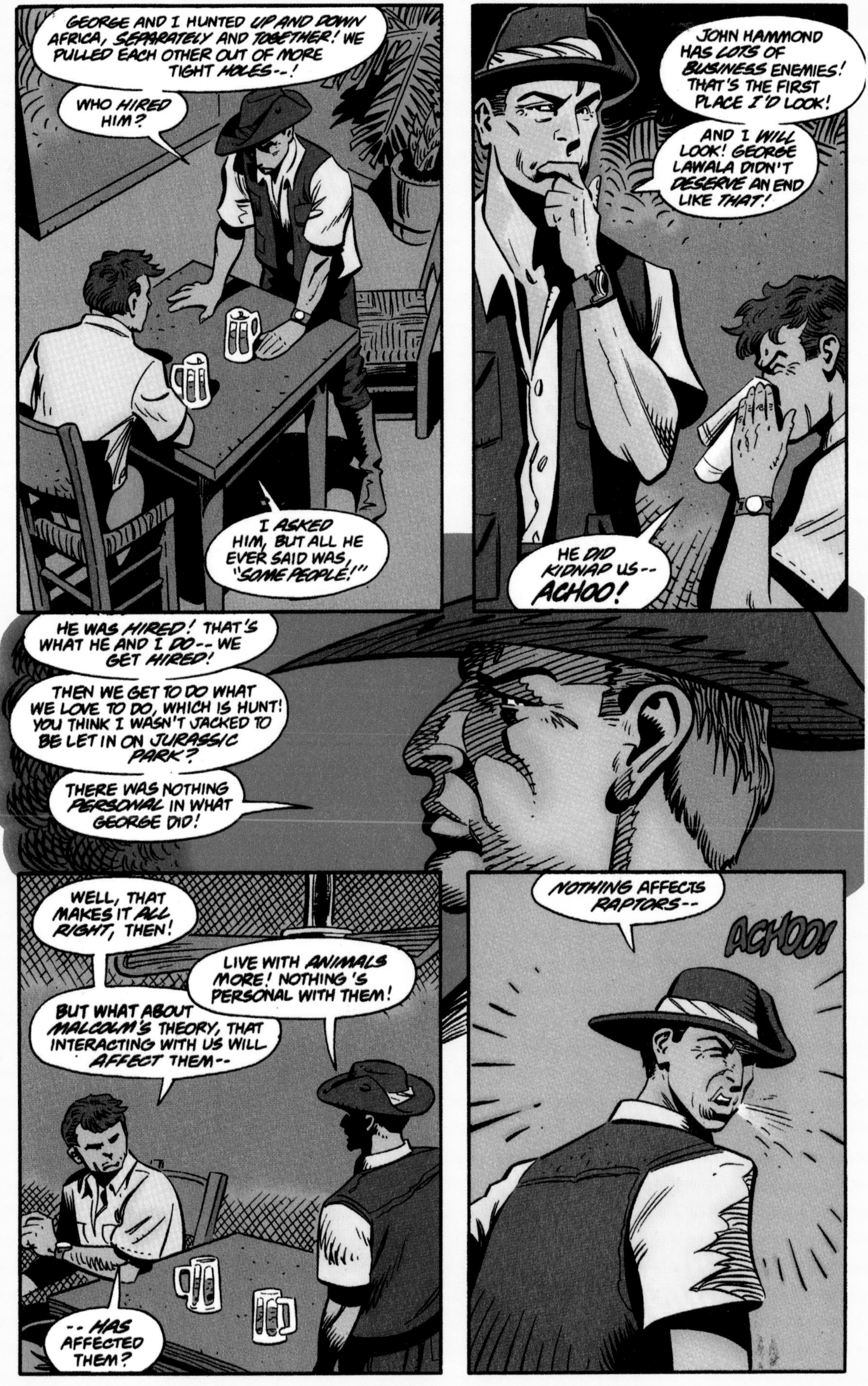
GEORGE AND I HUNTED UP AND DOWN AFRICA, SEPARATELY AND TOGETHER! WE PULLED EACH OTHER OUT OF MORE TIGHT HOLES--!
WHO HIRED HIM?
I ASKED HIM, BUT ALL HE EVER SAID WAS, "SOME PEOPLE!"
JOHN HAMMOND HAS LOTS OF BUSINESS ENEMIES! THAT'S THE FIRST PLACE I'D LOOK!
AND I WILL LOOK! GEORGE LAWALA DIDN'T DESERVE AN END LIKE THAT!
HE DID KIDNAP US-- ACHOO!
HE WAS HIRED! THAT'S WHAT HE AND I DO-- WE GET HIRED!
THEN WE GET TO DO WHAT WE LOVE TO DO, WHICH IS HUNT! YOU THINK I WASN'T JACKED TO BE LET IN ON JURASSIC PARK?
THERE WAS NOTHING PERSONAL IN WHAT GEORGE DID!
WELL, THAT MAKES IT ALL RIGHT, THEN!
LIVE WITH ANIMALS MORE! NOTHING'S PERSONAL WITH THEM!
BUT WHAT ABOUT MALCOLM'S THEORY, THAT INTERACTING WITH US WILL AFFECT THEM--
--HAS AFFECTED THEM?
NOTHING AFFECTS RAPTORS--
ACHOO!

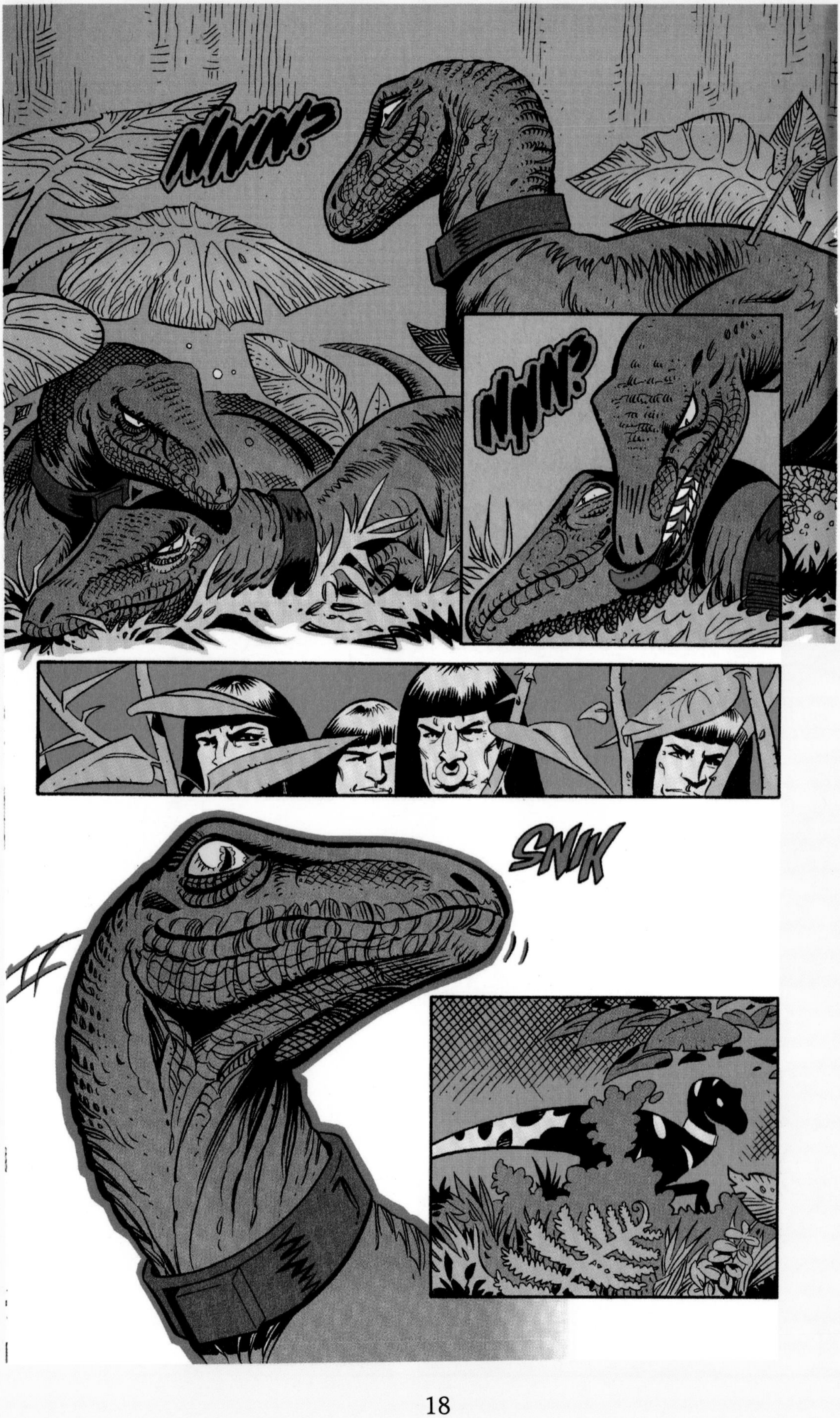
NNN?
NNN?
SNIK

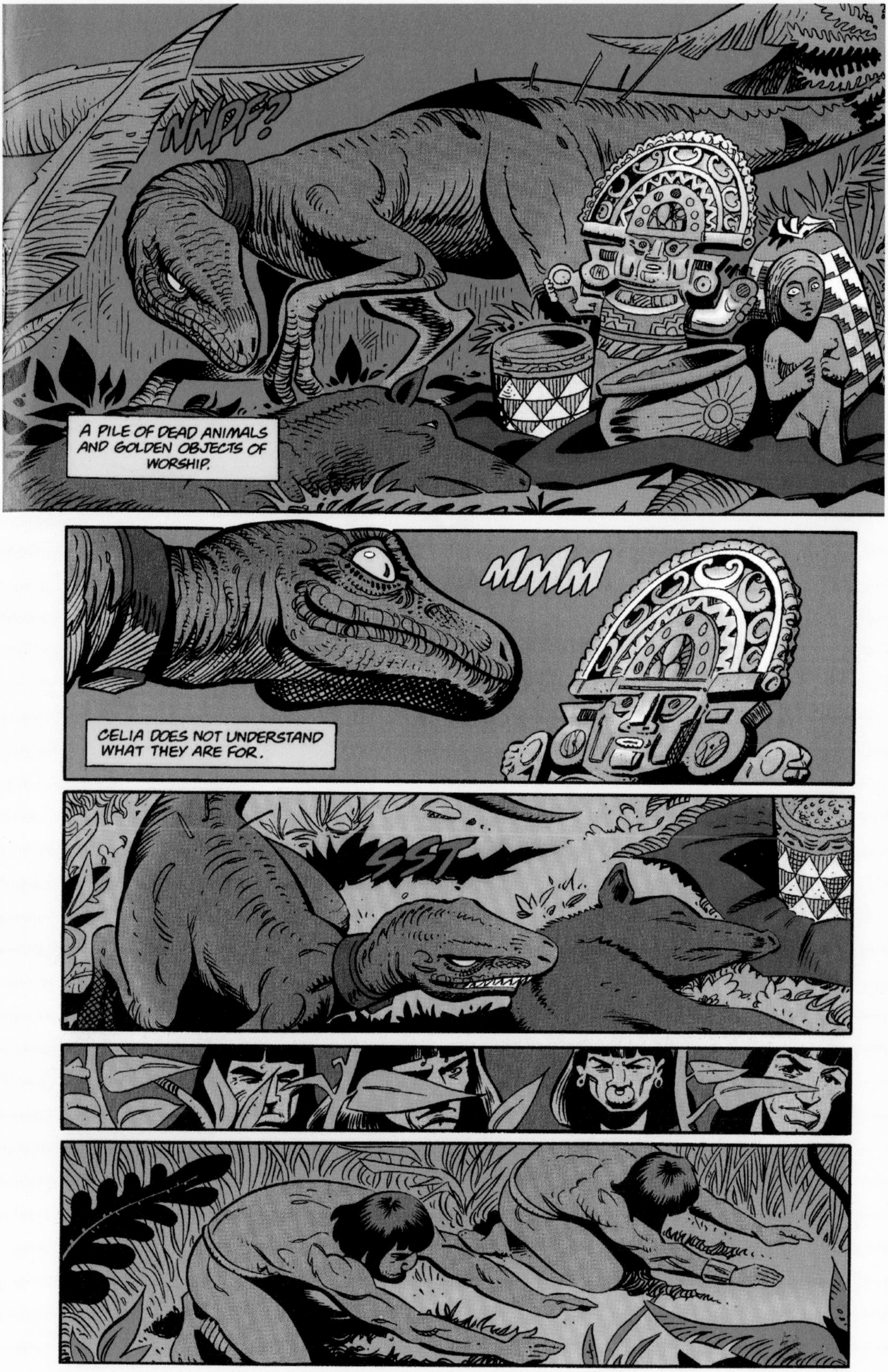
NNPF?
A PILE OF DEAD ANIMALS AND GOLDEN OBJECTS OF WORSHIP.
MMM
CELIA DOES NOT UNDERSTAND WHAT THEY ARE FOR.
SST

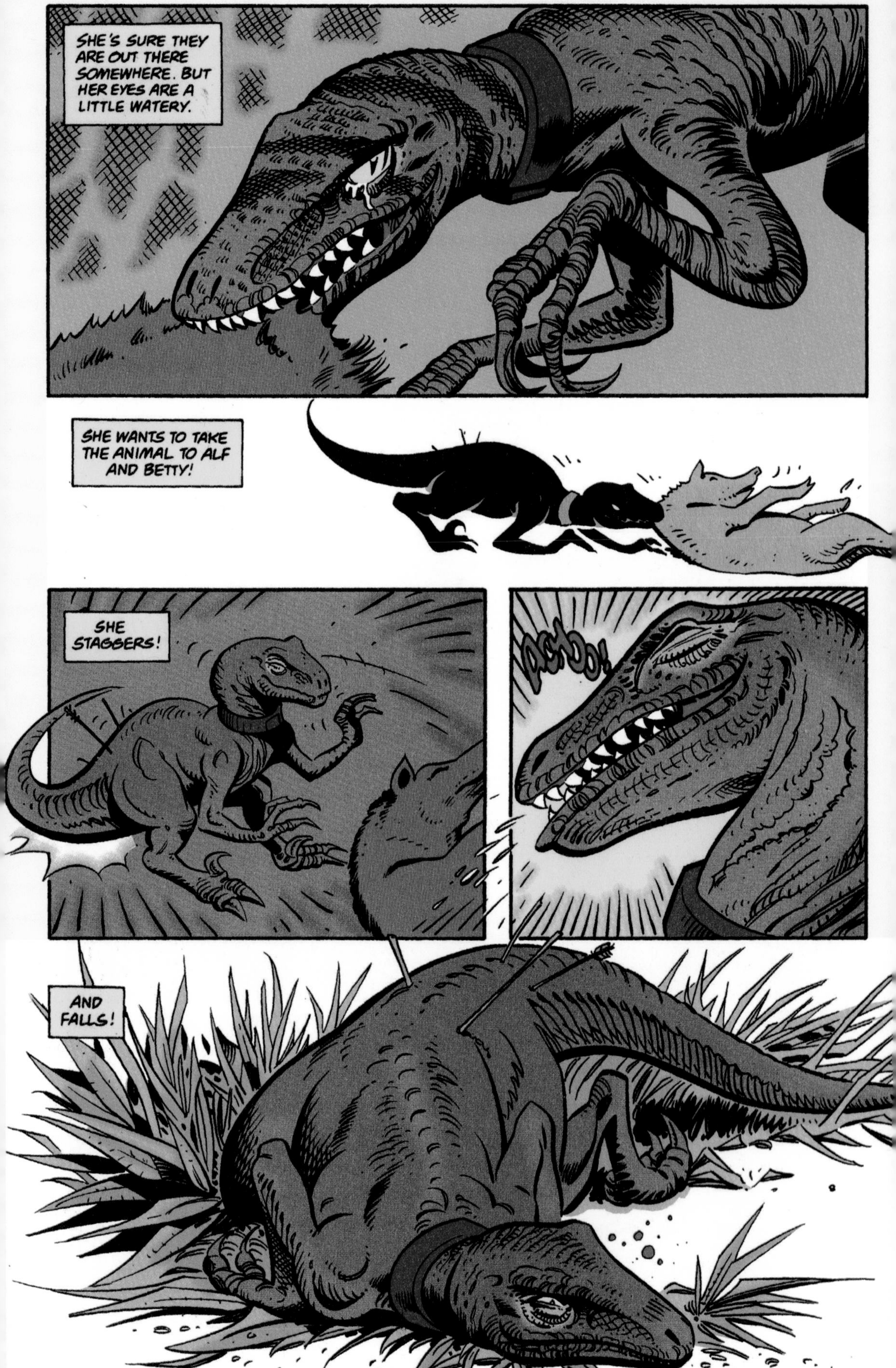
SHE'S SURE THEY ARE OUT THERE SOMEWHERE. BUT HER EYES ARE A LITTLE WATERY.
SHE WANTS TO TAKE THE ANIMAL TO ALF AND BETTY!
SHE STAGGERS!
AND FALLS!

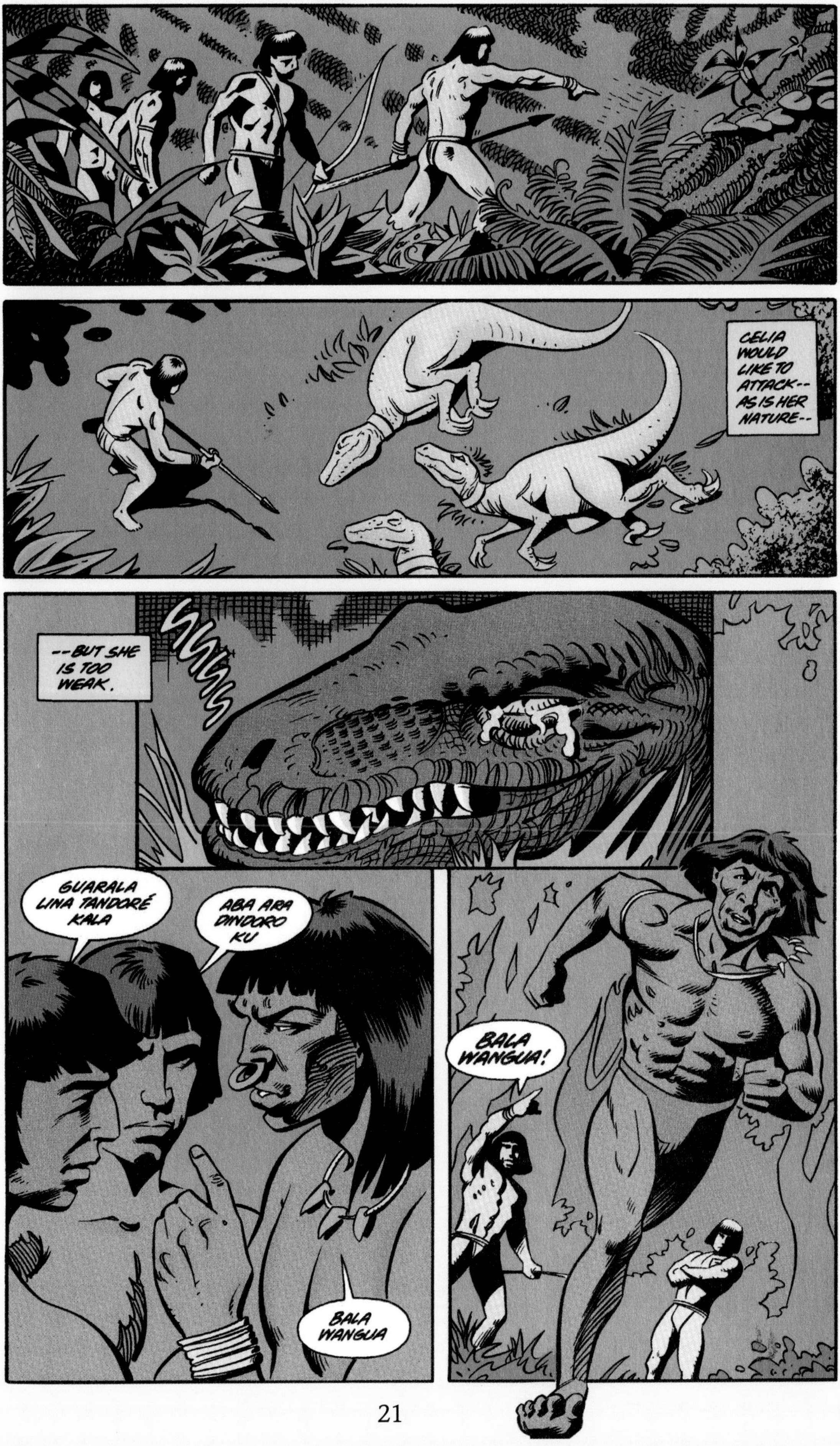
CELIA WOULD LIKE TO ATTACK-- AS IS HER NATURE--
--BUT SHE IS TOO WEAK.
GUARALA LINA TANDORÉ KALA
ABA ARA DINDORO KU
BALA WANGUA
BALA WANGUA!

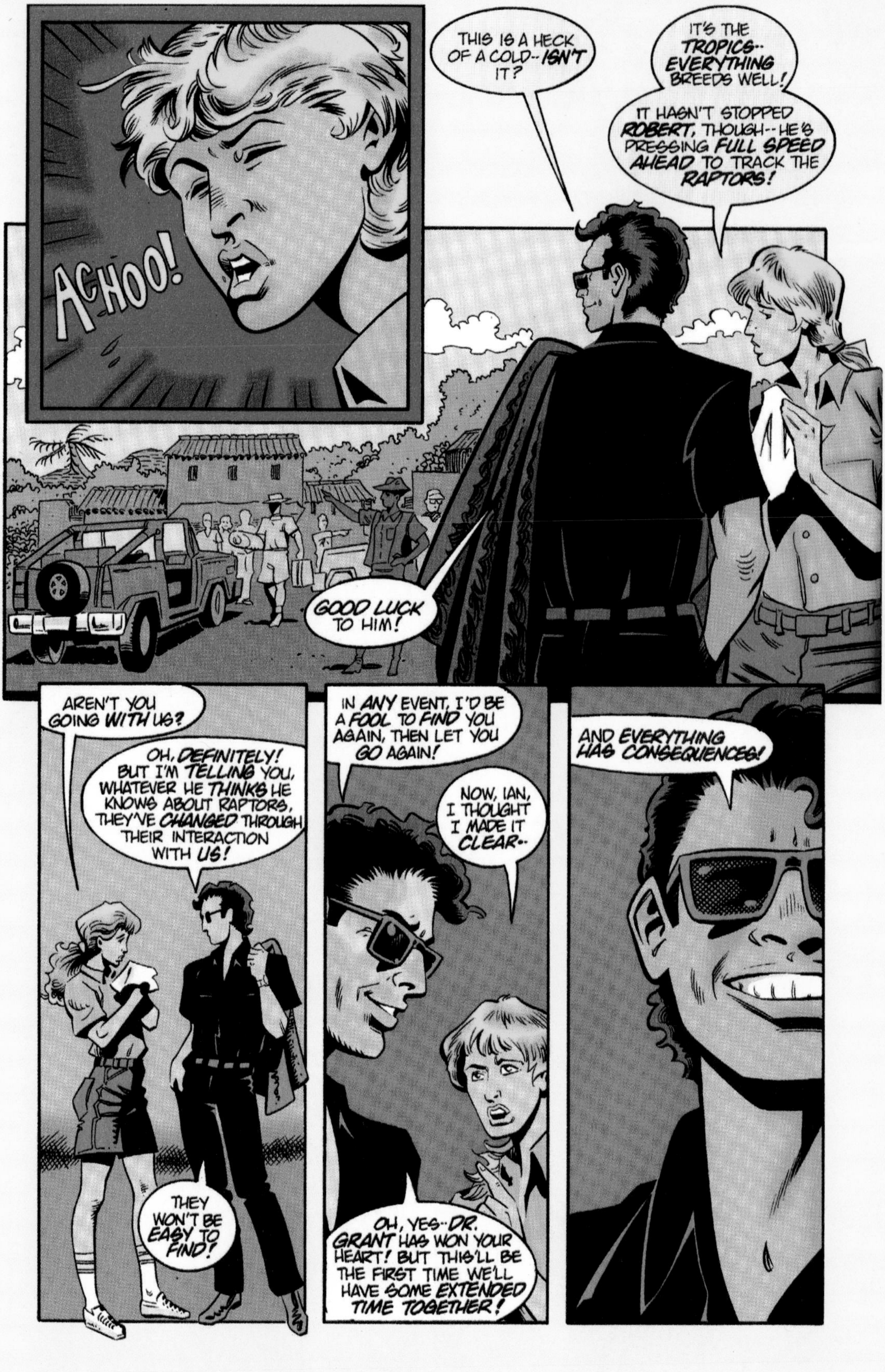
ACHOO!
THIS IS A HECK OF A COLD--ISN'T IT?
IT'S THE TROPICS-- EVERYTHING BREEDS WELL!
IT HASN'T STOPPED ROBERT, THOUGH--HE'S PRESSING FULL SPEED AHEAD TO TRACK THE RAPTORS!
GOOD LUCK TO HIM!
AREN'T YOU GOING WITH US?
OH, DEFINITELY! BUT I'M TELLING YOU, WHATEVER HE THINKS HE KNOWS ABOUT RAPTORS, THEY'VE CHANGED THROUGH THEIR INTERACTION WITH US!
THEY WON'T BE EASY TO FIND!
IN ANY EVENT, I'D BE A FOOL TO FIND YOU AGAIN, THEN LET YOU GO AGAIN!
NOW, IAN, I THOUGHT I MADE IT CLEAR--
OH, YES--DR. GRANT HAS WON YOUR HEART! BUT THIS'LL BE THE FIRST TIME WE'LL HAVE SOME EXTENDED TIME TOGETHER!
AND EVERYTHING HAS CONSEQUENCES!

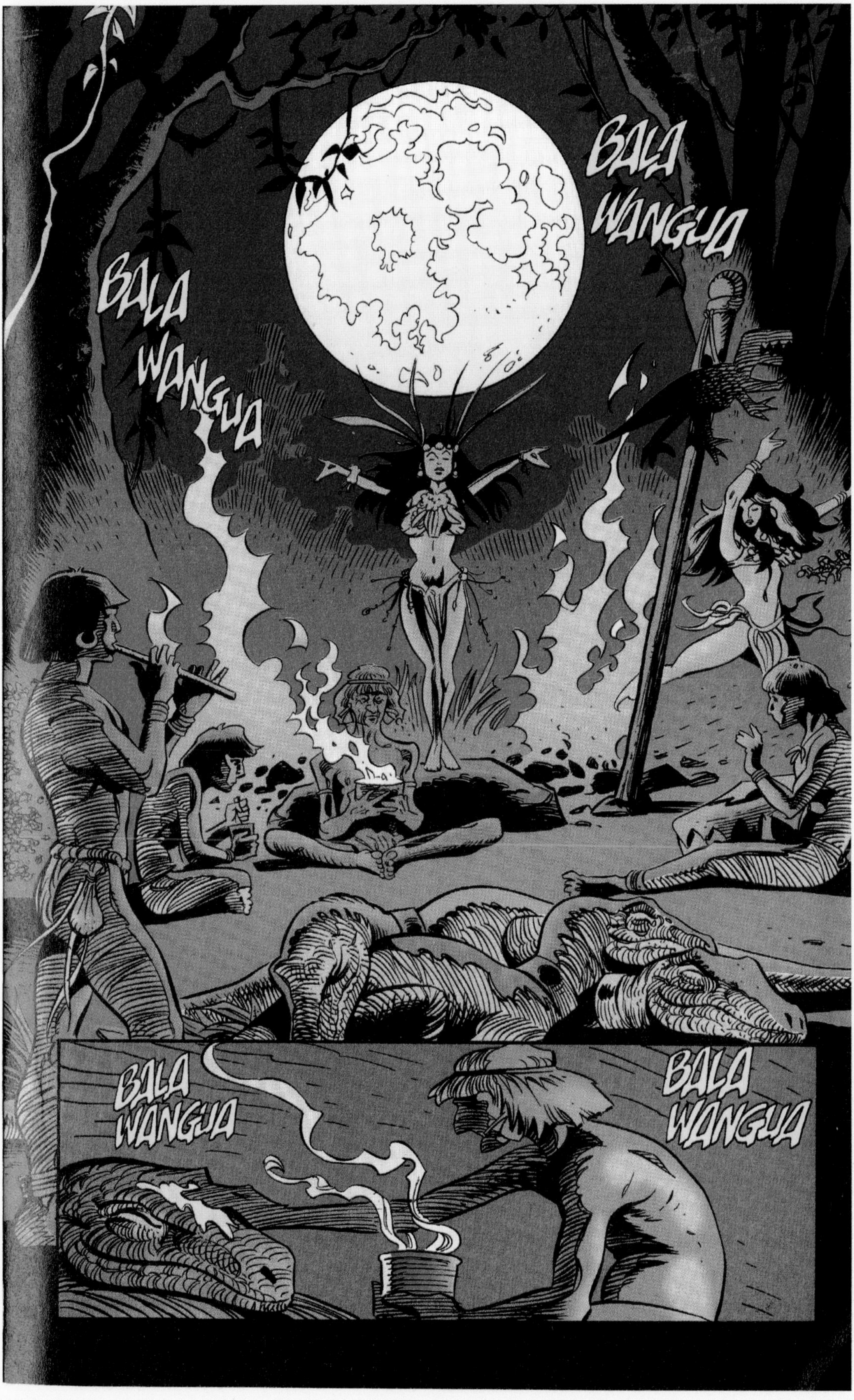
BALA WANGUA
BALA WANGUA
BALA WANGUA
BALA WANGUA

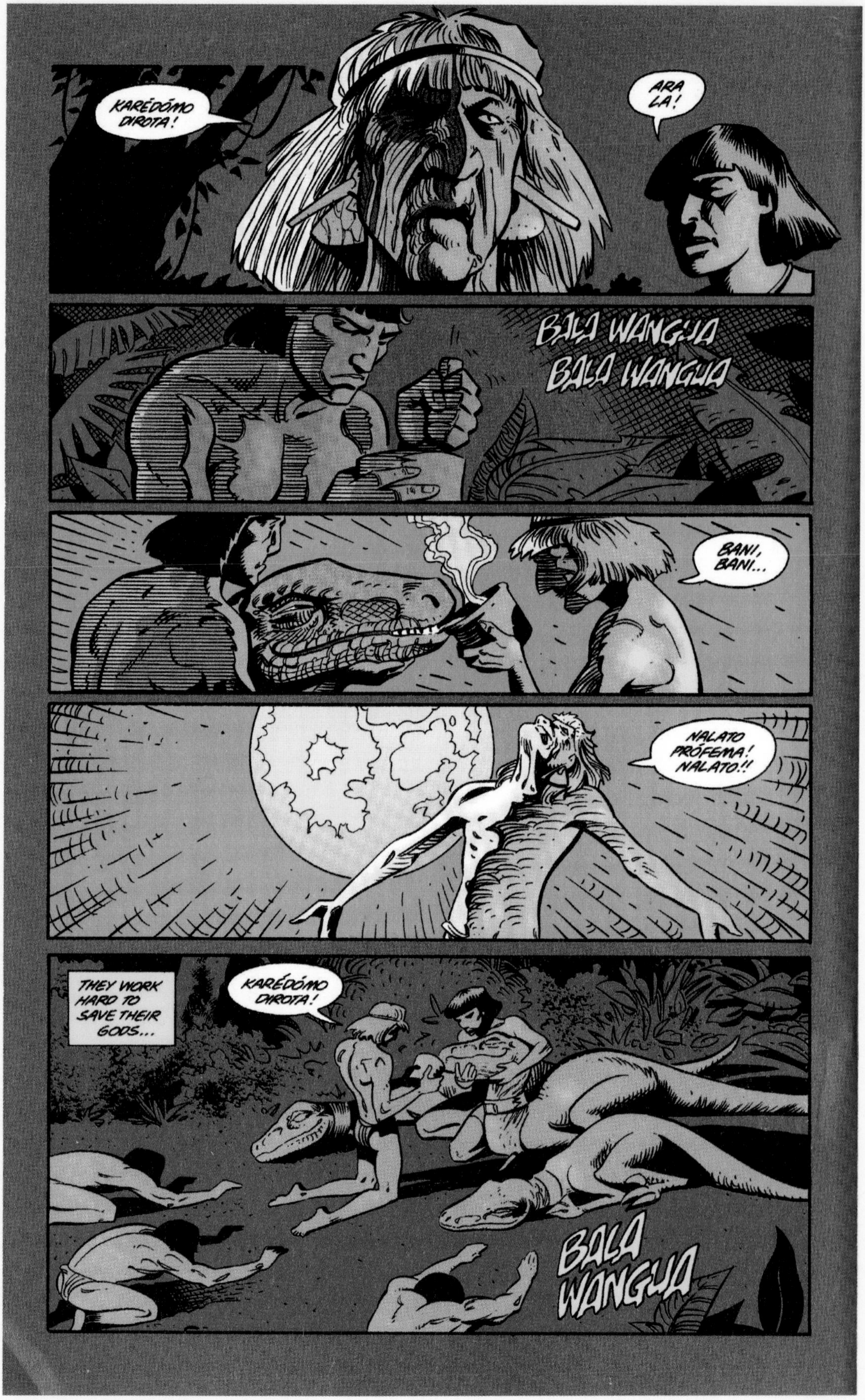
KARÉDÓMO DIROTA!
ARA LA!
BALA WANGUA
BALA WANGUA
BANI, BANI...
NALATO PRÓFEMA! NALATO!!
THEY WORK HARD TO SAVE THEIR GODS...
KARÉDÓMO DIROTA!
BALA WANGUA

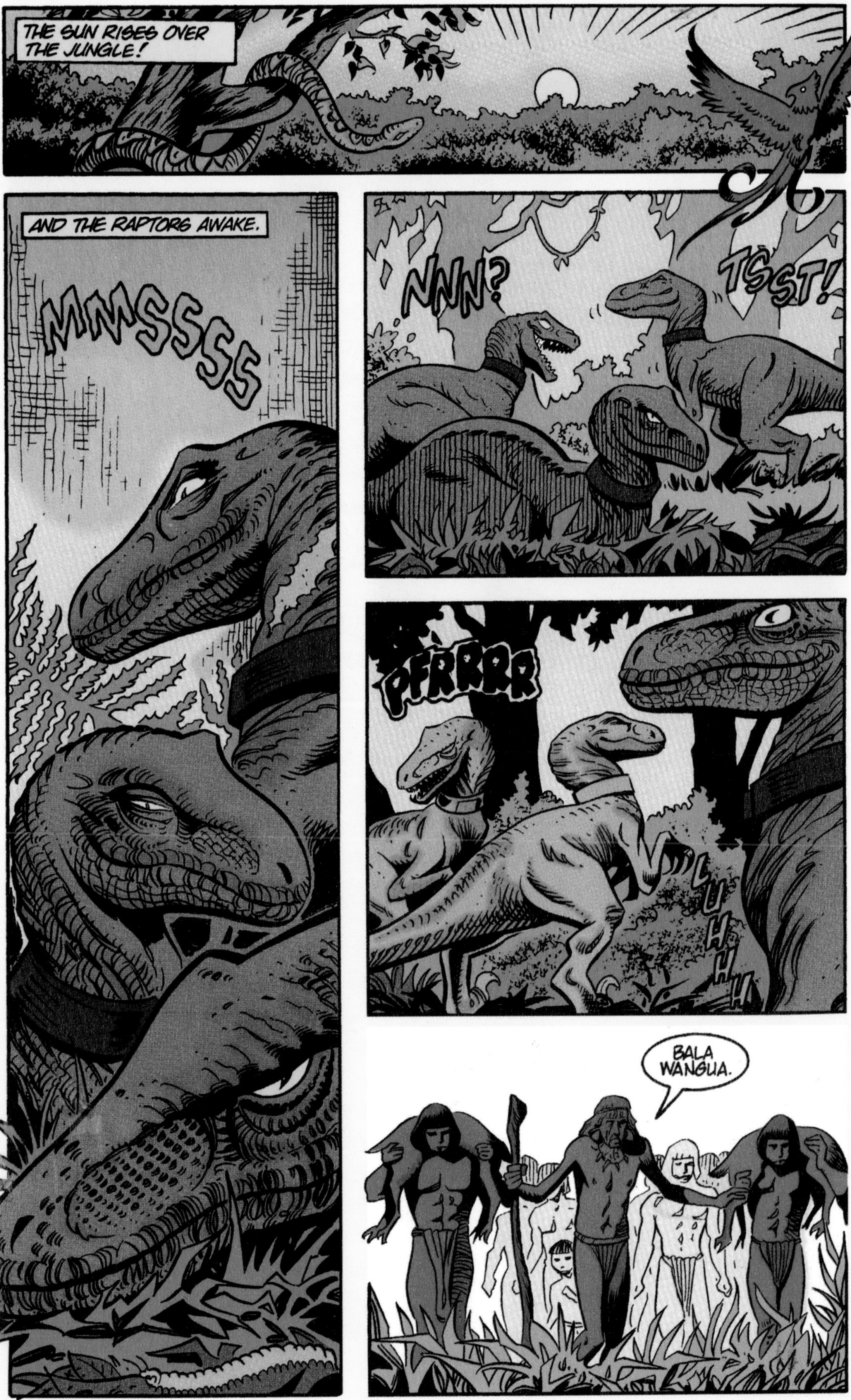
THE SUN RISES OVER THE JUNGLE!
AND THE RAPTORS AWAKE.
MMSSSSS
NNN?
TSSST!
PFRRRR
UHHH
BALA WANGUA.

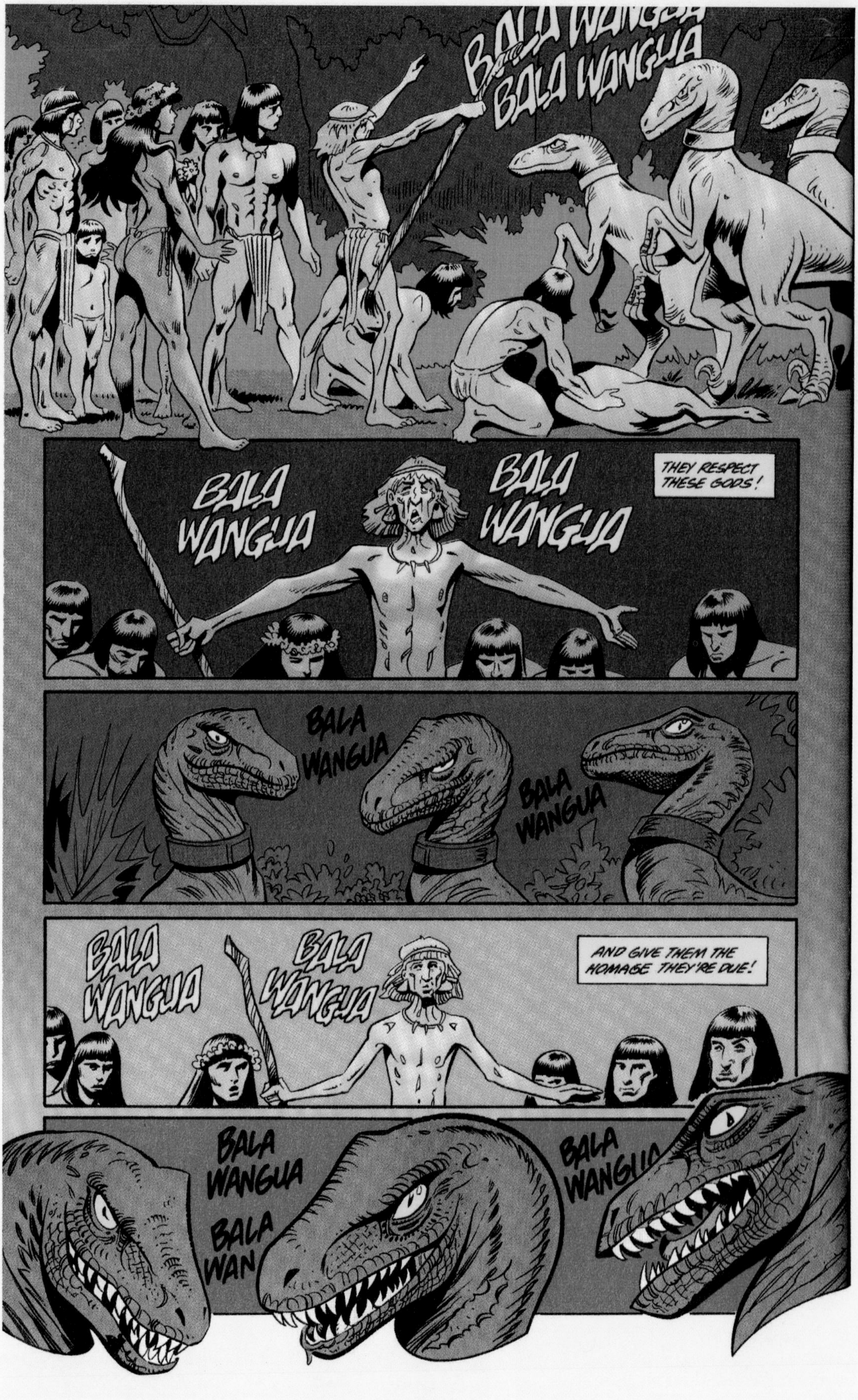
BALA WANGUA
BALA WANGUA
BALA WANGUA
BALA WANGUA
THEY RESPECT THESE GODS!
BALA WANGUA
BALA WANGUA
BALA WANGUA
BALA WANGUA
AND GIVE THEM THE HOMAGE THEY'RE DUE!
BALA WANGUA
BALA WAN
BALA WANGUA

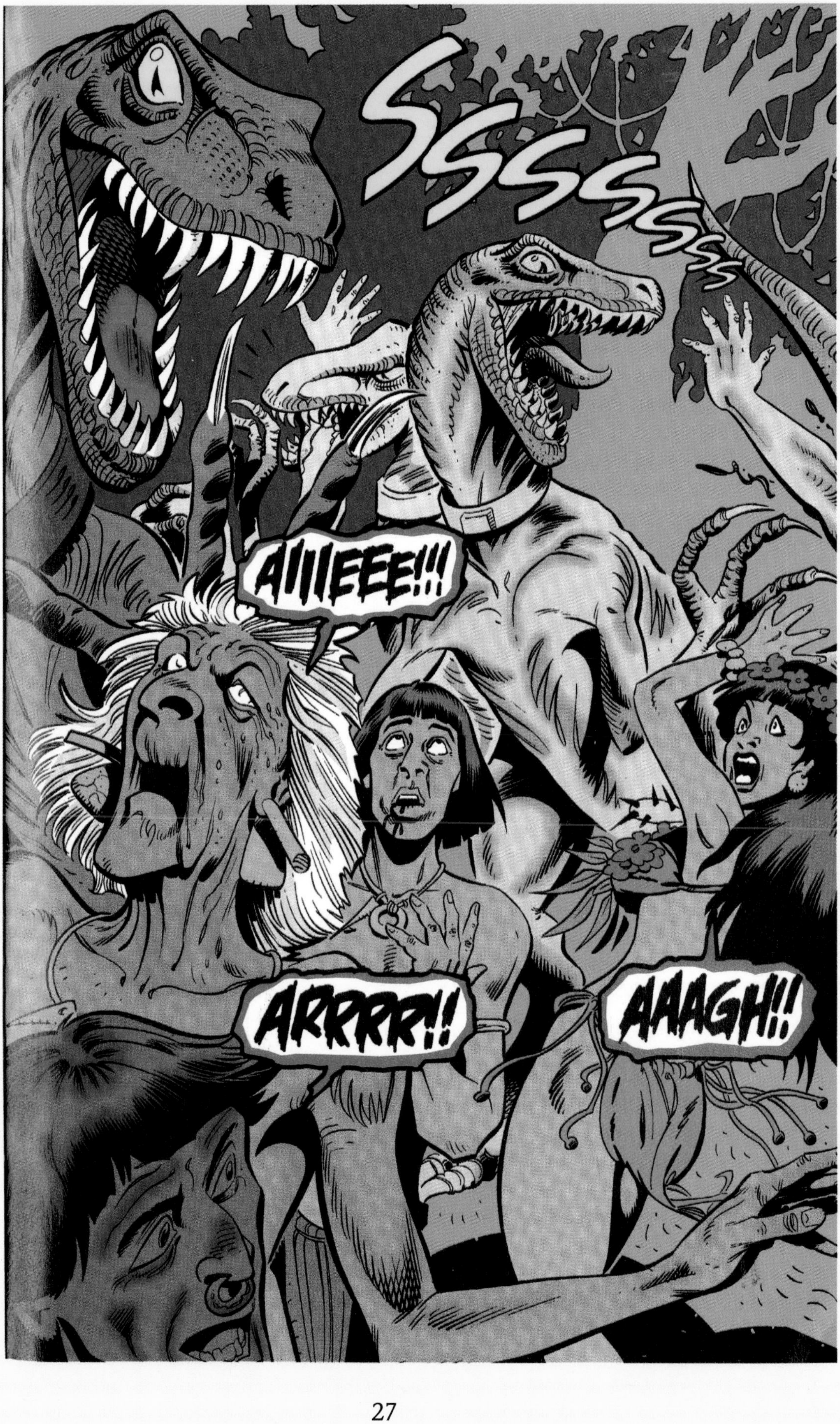
SSSSSSSSS
AIIIEEE!!!
ARRRR!!
AAAGH!!

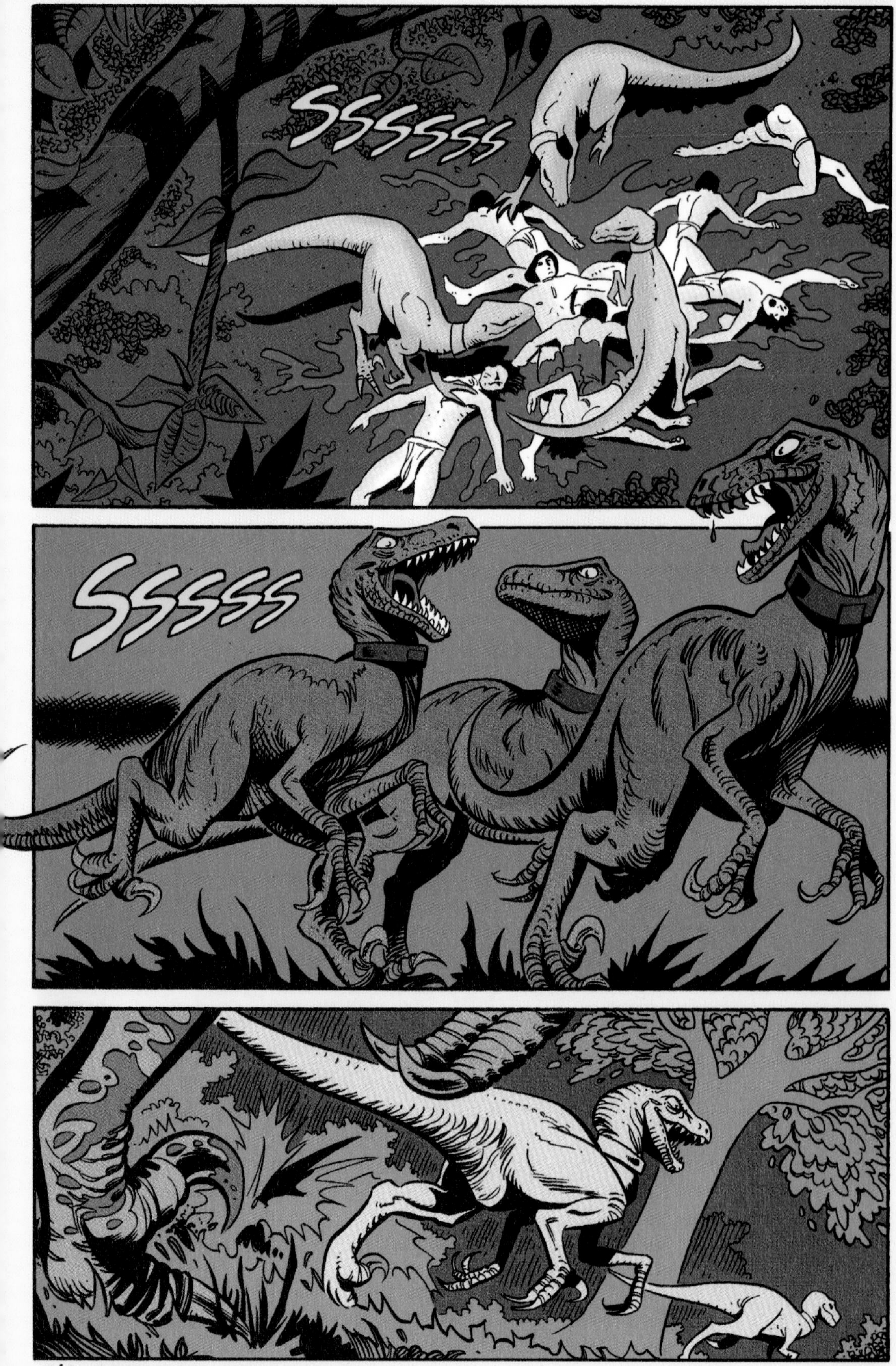
SSSSSS
SSSSS

IT'S GOOD TO BE *FREE AND WILD* AGAIN...

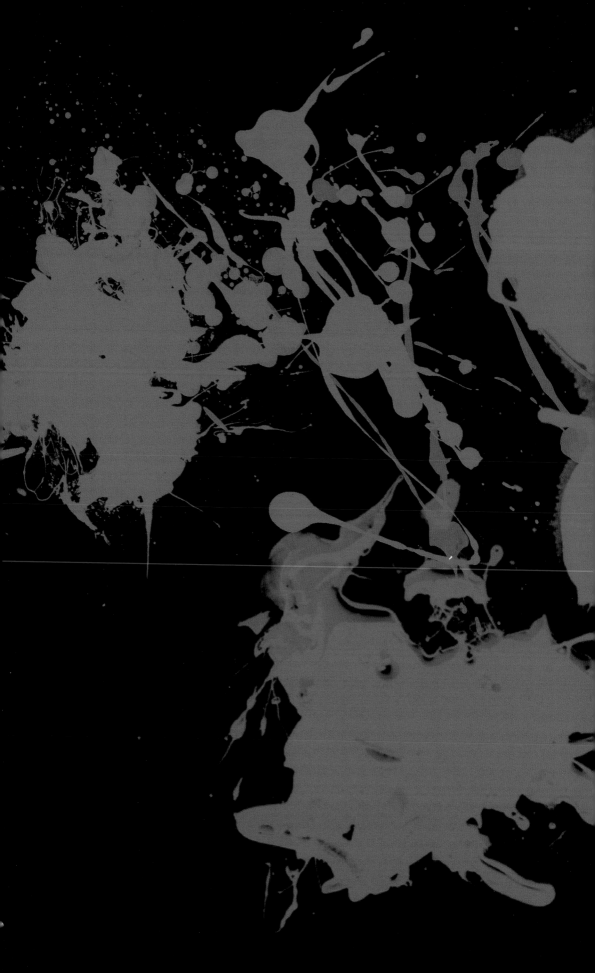